The Hedonist of Hollow Hill

By: K.R. Young

This book is a work of fiction. References to real people, events, establishments, organizations, or locales are intended only to provide a sense of authenticity and are used fictitiously. All other characters, and all incidents and dialogue, are drawn from the author's imagination and are not to be construed as real.

THE HEDONIST OF HOLLOW HILL © 2024 by K.R. Young. All rights reserved. No part of this book may be used or reproduced in any manner whatsoever without written permission except in the case of brief quotations embodied in critical articles and reviews.

ISBN: 979-8-30-190279-6

This book is dedicated to all the young mamas out there.. You can do anything.

Prologue

Welcome to Hollow Hill, Kentucky. Where everyone knows everyone. The biggest attractions in this town is Gorin Ridge and the neighboring town of Doveport. Doveport is alot bigger than Hollow Hill and has a lot more tourist traffic. The only thing we're known for is the disappearances of a few high school girls in the late 2010's. I think I found one of them.

It sucks I have to work on my eighteenth birthday. I should be partying with Dad and Lila, not working at Full Moon Diner. At least Ophelia is letting me wear a birthday girl sticker on my uniform.

This double shift is going slow. The man I had this morning is back again.

He greets me with the same smile from before. I take out my pad and pen; I greet him with the same smile. "What can I get for you, sir?"

"I'll take a cup of coffee and a roast beef Manhattan" he says, taking off his sunglasses. He's still wearing a surgical mask. These days, you can't be too careful. It's a nice summer afternoon and the sun has been baking the pavement.

"Alright, anything else?" I ask, looking into his eyes. There's something dark about them.

"I'll have a piece of today's special pie. The pie case looks really good." he says.

"Okay, I'll have your coffee for you as soon as possible." I say, walking away from the table.

I go to the server line and make his coffee; I make a small bowl of sugar and grab some creamer.

Today's special is pumpkin pie, I mean it is October after all. Lila bursts in and greets me loud enough to be heard down the street.

"Hey Mia, what's up?" she says, sitting in her usual spot. She sits on the high bar right in front of the server line.

"Nothing much, I got a good looking guy in blue today. He's been in here twice." I whisper, putting his coffee on my tray.

"Damn, he must like you." she winks.

"Nah, he doesn't even know my name." I wave her off.

"Happy birthday anyway. Hey, I got you something." she says, digging a gift bag out from behind her.

"Okay, just set it on the bar, I'll get it when I come back." I tell her as I round the corner with the tray.

Joel yells from the kitchen.

"Food's up for Mia!"

I go to the man's table and drop off his coffee.

"Thank you, Mia." the man says my name as if he's known me my whole life.

"You're welcome, sir." I say, putting the sugar on the table and turning to retrieve his food. The sandwich is piping hot and smells delicious. I hope Ophelia lets me take my break soon, after handling this plate I'm really hungry.

As I drop the food off at the man's table,he grabs my wrist .

"Do you want to run away with me? You're such a pretty gal." he says, staring me straight in the eyes.

I snatch my arm away from him. "No, you creep. Get off me!"

"Why not, little rabbit?" he says, I can tell his mask is hiding a sinister smile. I have to get away from him.

"Because, I have to be home to do my homework. I'm only 16.." I snap.

Being "mature" for my age sure does suck sometimes.

"Oh, I didn't know you were that young. I'm sorry."

*****

The man looks like he's about to explode with anger. He's tapping his leg, and gripping his coffee cup really tight. I turn to walk away and I hear a shatter and scream of agony. I turn back to find him holding a bloody hand and cursing.

"Oh my God. Are you okay?"

"Hell no, I'm not okay. Ah fuck, this hurts." he mutters , using the napkin beside him to wipe away the blood.

"Ophelia! We need the first aid kit!" I yell.

Ophelia, the owner, races to the front line, "My Lord, what happened?"

The man looks at me, his expression completely different now that she's here, and then explains that he was gripping his coffee cup a little too tight.

"Them cups are real fragile. I'm sorry, sir. Let me get you cleaned up," Ophelia frets, shooing me away. "Go take a break, Mia."

"Yes ma'am." I nod, backing away toward the bar.

"What happened over there?" Lila asks, craning to get a better look.

"Old dude got mad that I didn't want to run away with him, so he busted the coffee cup in his hand." I explain, sitting beside her on one of the swiveling stools. Joel comes to the front and gruffly asks what I want to eat.

"I'll take an omelet with ham and broccoli. Can you get me a cup of coffee since you're back there?"

"Yeah, no problem kiddo. Happy birthday." Joel says, handing me a crumpled up $20.

"Thanks, man! I'll add it to my tip jar." I grin over the counter at him. My jar is close to overflowing today, since I'm the only one working both shifts because Julie called out.

Joel pours me a cup of coffee.

"Any sugar or cream?"

"Nah, I drink it black."

"Ooh, tough girl." Joel jokes.

"So, why did that guy ask you to run away?" Lila asks, still trying to catch a glimpse of the carnage I caused.

"The creep thought I was of age. Like that would make a difference.."

"Oh, ew. Anyway, open your present!" she eagerly dismisses the incident and changes the subject. I grab the bag and rip out the tissue paper. It's a little rectangular box and a bag of my favorite candy. I open the box and it's a shiny new pocket knife.

"I can't have this here." I whisper, shoving it back into the bag.

"I know, but you need something for self defense since you walk home every night."

"You're right. Thank you." I admit, slipping it into my apron instead .

"Well, chick, I gotta get home. Mr. Jensen's cat isn't gonna feed himself." Lila hops off her seat and turns to leave. Mr. Jensen is an older man that lives beside her. He's in the hospital and she's watching Phil for him.

"Alright, my break is almost up anyway. See ya."

Joel comes back up with my omelet and asks me if I want a refill.

"Yes, please. I'm starting to feel really tired." I yawn.

This omelet is amazing. The cheese is gooey, the ham is juicy and the broccoli is crisp. This is the first work birthday I've had, and this alone has made it worthwhile.

"How about a skillet cookie?" Joel offers.

"I would love one, but I don't have time. My break is almost up."

"Shame. I'll get you one the next time you work, okay?"

"Okay, thanks Joel." I stack my dishes and toss my trash before returning to duty.

Meanwhile, the man jumps up after Ophelia cleans him off. He slams a bloodied hundred dollar bill on the bar and practically runs out the door.

Ophelia shrugs it off and comes up to the high bar to meet me.

"Hey, did he tip you that hundred?"

Ophelia stares down at it.

"Yeah but it's bloody. Yuck." I grumble, pointing at the bloodied bill.

"Given the situation, I'm surprised he didn't leave you more. He spoke very highly of you. He said that you're very sweet. I'll get you a crisp one out of the safe." she says, disappearing into her office

"Okay."

"It's time for you to go home, babygirl. You've been here damn near all day." she hands me the new bill and ushers me toward the exit.

"Alright. Just keep my tips from today and put them in my locker."

"I will."

I grab my bag from under the server line and get my hoodie from my locker. I hug Ophelia, wave to Joel and head home like I do every other shift. But tonight, as I'm walking out the door, I notice the man from earlier still lingering in the dark parking lot. He snaps his head up to glare at me and begins skulking my way.

"Hello, little rabbit. I got something for you." he snarls,

grabbing me harshly by the hair and injecting something into my neck before I can react.

I suddenly feel really sleepy as he throws me over his shoulder. I feel my body being put in a trunk, but I see it from a distance like I'm watching a horror movie starring myself. My head lolls and bobs as he drives away.

I wake up and I'm suspended by my wrists in some type of cellar. There's a wall of knives and other methods of torture. There's a faint ammonia smell. He comes down the stairs wearing a devil mask that covers his whole face.

"Look who's awake. Now it's time to really wake you up."

He grabs a whip and begins lashing my flesh. I scream in pain and beg him to stop. The lashes burn my skin as the tip of the whip cuts into me.

Once he was done, he stomped back up the stairs, leaving me to whimper and bleed out. After he was gone, I took a closer look at how I was suspended. All I was tied up with was some frayed rope. Like a fox caught in a snare, I use my teeth and tear my way out of the restraint. Groaning in pain from my fall, I stagger to my feet and run out the first door I find. I sneak past the cabin window and flee into the woods beyond.

The cold air is nipping at my skin, burning like dry ice but I push on. As I pass through the trees, I hear him roar behind me. I make it to the clearing while branches break behind me. I run harder than I ever have before. Miraculously, I make it to town. But the streets are dead and no one is out.

I fill my lungs and start to sprint across the parking lot of the grocery store. It must be at least midnight. I need to make it to Mama's. I doubt she'll believe me but I need someone I know now more than ever.

I make it to mama's in what feels like an eternity, I run up the steps and bang on the door. Mama opens the door in her nightgown with her eyes half open. "Girl, what the hell happened to you?" "There's a man in a devil mask trying to get me!" I scream, running inside and hiding. I fall against the wall and slide down, sobbing. Leona, my older sister, comes down the stairs and asks Mama what happened.

"I don't know, she must have done some sort of drug, she's acting crazy. I'm taking her to the hospital. She needs to be evaluated." Mama says coldly. She assumes that because of my past with drug use. Not to mention my past of seeing ghosts.

"Evaluated?! She's got cuts all over her! She's been hurt bad." Leona screams. She comes to my side and hugs me. I wince in pain but lean in for the embrace. She rocks with me and tells me everything will be alright. They'll get whoever did this to me, I'm safe now.

But it wasn't alright. And I wasn't safe. Not with Mama.

The next morning I got sent to Westbrook Psychiatric Hospital.

Chapter One: Westbrook

(2 years later)

Arriving at Dr. Edmundson's office, I pause, take my normal deep breath and release it. Opening the door and stepping inside, the interior is classic academia. Chairs are strategically placed around the waiting room to keep anyone from feeling boxed in or trapped. Taking a seat, I wave at her secretary. Westbrook Psychiatric Hospital became my home away from home for the past two years after my attack. Dr. Edmundson is my psychiatrist and is helping me cope with what happened. Or, she's trying to anyway.

"Dr. Edmundson will see you now, Mia." called Nurse Beverly.

Walking into the now open office door, I see overflowing bookshelves lining the walls surrounding a big cherry oak desk in the middle of the room. Her office always smells like heavy incense and cherries.

Dr. Edmundson is conventionally beautiful; blonde hair, bright green eyes and rosy pink lips. She is like a mother to me.

I casually lie down on the doctor's chaise-lounge and close my eyes. Again taking a deep breath, I relax all of my muscles as I exhale, releasing a small sigh of contentment.

"Have you had any symptoms?" Dr. Edmundson said

"I haven't had any hallucinations, no." I said

"You do understand that lying to me isn't going to help you, right?" she said.

"I do see a strange woman in my dreams. But that's about it." I said, thinking of the woman in all black.

"What does she look like?" she asked.

"Black hair, blue eyes, pale skin."

"Okay. What does she do in your dream?"

"She is asking me to help her. She guides me to the river and I wake up."

"Do you think it's a ghost?" she asked.

"Yes. She looks like a friend of my sister's."

"Okay," she said, writing on her legal pad.

"Your test results came back from your last evaluation" she continues.

"Okay? And?"

"You're clear to go."

"Clear to go? What if he kills me this time?"

"Mia, I understand your fear but it's time for you to go back into the world."

"But I-" My body began to shake at the possibility of going home.

"You'll be living with your mother, correct?"

"I guess so, but."

"Great. You'll be leaving first thing tomorrow morning."

"But I don't feel comfortable living with my mom. I'd rather live with my dad."

"Your father is a recovering alcoholic. That's not the best idea."

My dad, Michael, has been in recovery for the past year and a half. He started to drink when he and Mama were having marital issues. The first six months of me being here, he started to sober up.

It scared him half to death knowing that I was almost killed. He's the only one that believed me. But my mom, Winona, will be the best option for my recovery, at least for now. Guess I don't have much of a choice, do I?

Look out world, Mia's coming back to town…hopefully without incident this time.

Chapter Two: Homecoming

Waking up to the morning sun peeking into my room, I'm hoping I'm truly ready to go home and face any demons that follow me there. The ride is three hours from the hospital to home; the driver was dropping off other patients in the van with me. They were either going home or being taken to another facility in their home counties. After dropping off a couple of other passengers the next town over, we finally arrived at Harlan Court where my mom's house is. It's a sight for sore eyes and terrifying at the same time. It's a small two-story house that's been painted in a rainbow of colors. Pulling into the driveway, I see Leona jumping around and waving.

She turns and yells into the house. "Hey Mia's here!" Running right off the porch, she runs into the side of the car as it comes to a stop. Once she manages to get my door open, she wraps me in a tight hug. Her long embrace is a near-suffocating bear hug, but I'm alright with that.

I see Mama over Leona's shoulder as she walks out of the house. She's a tall woman with graying braids. Her mahogany skin shines in the morning sun. She never called to see how I was. I resent her for that. She sent me to hell.

"I like what you did with your hair, it looks good." she mutters awkwardly. Compliments were always hard to pry from her.

"One of the care techs took the time to do it. It took three of her shifts to finish them." I say as I look at the ends of my box braids. The air is uncomfortably still for a moment. Mama finally speaks. "You going to go back to Full Moon Diner to work?" she asks, she's all about her girls having financial independence.

"Yeah, I'll give Ophelia a call when I get done unpacking." I tell her.

"Alright, let's get you in the house and out of… that." she says, looking at the scrubs they sent me home in. My original clothes were torn to shreds when I got to the hospital.

Mama stops walking and turns to face me before we make it inside. "Oh, someone is here to see you." She barely opens the door and it's Lila. She runs out the door so fast I'm afraid she's going to mow me down. "Mia! I missed you!"

"Lila, girl, you came to see me a couple weeks ago." I laugh, trying to hold us both up.

"I know, but this is different. I can actually hug you now!" she squeals.

I cherish every embrace, despite my protests. This is the first real human contact in two years. Mama stayed away due to the *'no touch'* rule. She's a hugger, believe it or not, and I love her for it. Leona came and visited me to see how I was doing, but we both struggled with it. Lila managed to contain herself, as she was my eyes on the outside and couldn't afford to get blacklisted. That girl told me all the goings on at school while I was "staying with my dad".

Apparently, there's a gorgeous new chemistry teacher, but she doesn't go on about him for long. The old chemistry professor, Mr. Cheadle, had retired. She knows there's only one man for me at the high school.

Lila tells me about the fights that Karol and Jesse have somehow stayed together through.
Karol is Jesse's girlfriend. She's an obnoxious bitch. She's tall, skinny, and blonde. Jesse is on the college football team. I have a huge crush on him. I have ever since the ninth grade.
A little while later, I unpack my bags and spend time with Leona and Mama. Lila stays for supper and we catch up. She tells me how college

is a lot different than high school. I did college courses while I was in Westbrook. I'm a sophomore in college now.

After what seems to be the longest day, it's time for bed. Going to bed is easy and drifting off to sleep is even easier.

Chapter Three: The Dream and the Ghost

My dreams are always strange. The days I wake up from one of those vivid nights, I experience a piece of it. A conversation, certain people, something always plays out the way it does in my dream. Some of my dreams are like deja vu in the worst way. I'm running from him again, hearing his horrid voice taunting that me he would get me this time. The farther I ran from him, the more distorted and deep his voice became. The forest grew thinner and thinner until I came to a clearing. It was Lover's Lookout. Below me in the crashing water, a woman in a sinking car screams for help. She had long black hair and blue eyes; she was absolutely beautiful. Devil mask is behind me. I jump into the water to try to save the woman in the car and to escape him, but she was already submerged. I look up to see him glowering down at the lake. He takes off his mask but his face is obscured by the water in my eyes. I dive back down into the waves.

The woman pounded the window with her hand until her last breath, and I woke up in a cold sweat.

The last fragment of my dream whispered in my ear, low and sweet.

You know where I am. Find me.

Please.

Chapter Four: The Cabin

"Mia, don't forget to call Ophelia." Mama said, pouring her coffee that morning.

"I won't, I'll call her right now." I say, waiting to get a cup of my own. The phone rings twice, and a familiar voice answers . "Thank you for calling Full Moon Diner, how can I help you?"

"Yes, this is Mia Audley."

"How have you been, babygirl?"

"I'm better now." It wasn't a whole truth or a whole lie, but it sounded better than either. "I was calling to see if I could get my job back." I ask with anticipation.

"Sure, girl! We missed you. You're one of the best waitresses we've had. Can you come in tonight?"

"Yes, I"ll be there."

As I prepare for work that night, I look at myself in the mirror and I feel like myself for once in a long time. Mom takes me to the diner and my shift begins.

I'm in the green section tonight and I hope to the heavens I make a lot of good tips. My old regulars come in and they're put in my section. It's an elderly couple named Nelson and Edna Jenkins. "Hey

girlie! I haven't seen you in a long time!" Edna says, hugging me.
"It's good to be back. I missed y'all." I hug her back. "What can I get for y'all?" I ask, with my pen and order book ready.
"I'll have a Coke and water. I gotta flush my kidneys." Nelson replies , looking over his glasses.
"I'll have coffee and water." Edna says, putting her purse in the seat beside her.
"Okay, I'll be right back with your drinks." I hand them the menus so they can decide on their dinners. As I'm pouring Edna's coffee, Lila walks in. She sits at the high bar

in front of the server line just like we used to.

"Hey chick, what's up?" she says, looking at the menu like it's changed since before we were born.

"One second, Lil. I gotta take this order. Be right back." I give her a quick hug and scoot past, finishing Edna's coffee. I placed a creamer and sugar caddy on the tray and head to their table. "Y'all ready to order?"

"Yeah, I'll take the roast beef Manhattan." Edna says, handing me her menu back.

"I'll have the reuben sandwich with moon chips." Nelson says, doing the same.

I scribble down their order and put it in the POS to be sent to the kitchen. I fix myself a cup of coffee and get Lila a Mello Yello.

"So, what's up?" "You're good. I was just coming by to see you back in your element." Lila shrugs, opening her straw.

"Okay, do you want anything to eat?" I offer.

"Yeah, I'll take a baked potato with ham, broccoli, and cheese."

"Sounds good. I'm about to go on break, so I'll sit with you for a bit." I take a sip of my coffee.

"What day is today?" Lila asks; I see her not having a sense of time hasn't changed.

"Saturday. It's steak night." I remind her.

"Big money, huh?" she nudges me, taking a sip of her drink.

"Yeah, I can only hope. I mean, I want a car sometime this century." Joel yells from the back, breaking into the conversation. "Mia, your order's ready!"

"Be right back."

Or maybe not…

Ophelia sits a group in my section. *Oh well, at least I'm gonna make bank tonight,* I thought. Unfortunately, the group turns out to be Karol and her cronies. The only plus side is Jesse is with them. He's so good looking. He has black hair, hazel eyes, and a jawline that could cut diamonds.

"Mia, there's a group of four in your section!" Ophelia yells from the kitchen.

"Blissfully aware." I retort as I roll my eyes

As I walk up to the table, Jesse lights up. Karol and her cronies pay me no attention, because they are cackling at something or someone. I glance in the direction they're pointing, which is over to Nelson and Edna's table. Nelson has spilled his drink; he has Parkinson's disease and his tremors have gotten worse. I skip over the other teens and trot over to their table to give him the towel from my apron.

"Thank you, hon." he says as he's dabbling the Coke off of his shirt.

"Look at that old man! Isn't that pathetic?" Karol laughs behind her hand, though she isn't exactly quiet about it.

"It's not pathetic, Karol." snapsJesse, slamming his hand on the table.

Karol's laughing cuts short and her eyes widen. I walk back to their table and curtly ask for their orders. "What can I get for y'all?" Jesse only ordered a coffee. I go and put their order in the POS and get their drink orders ready.

"Here are your drinks, your food will be out shortly." I say, setting the drinks on the table. Jesse thanks me and winks. If I was a shade lighter, he'd see me blush.

I have a huge crush on him. But it's not an unrequited crush, he has a crush on me too. Too bad he's with Karol. When she found out that we liked each other, she snatched him up.

I walk back to the server line and find Lila staring at her phone.

She's too immersed in her memes to talk, so I let her be and go check on the food in the kitchen through the window.

"Hey Joel, how's the food coming?"

"It's almost ready, I'll holler when it's done." he grunts, chopping an onion and putting it in a saucepan.

"Okay." I say, putting my hands in my apron pocket.

A man in a suit comes in and sits at the high bar. He's rotund and tall. He asks for a piece of pie and a cup of coffee. I oblige and set it in front of him.

"Little lady, I have a question." he says in a gruff, low voice.

"Yes, sir?" I ask.

"Have you seen this woman?" he says, pulling a photo out of his pocket.

"No, sir." I say. That's the woman from my dream.

"Well, my team is working on her case. It's been cold for three years."

"I'm sorry, I hope you find her."

"I hope I do too, kid." he says. He puts a twenty on the bar and tells me to keep the change. Since Tanya called in, I've made almost a hundred dollars in the past three hours. It's going to be a good night. Lila puts her phone down and signals for me.

"I'm about to head out." she says, looking at the time.

"But your food isn't ready yet. Stay and eat, please?" I plead, giving her my best puppy eyes.

"Okay, fine. I'll stay and eat. But if that cat tears up my apartment, that's on you." she says, sitting back down.

"Mia, your potato is ready!" Joel yells from the cook line, putting the bowl in the window.

I hand it off to Lila and ask if she wants any butter and sour cream.

"2 butters, 3 sour creams. Please and thank you." she says, unrolling her cutlery.

"Mia, go on a fifteen! I'll watch your tables for ya!" Ophelia yells from the front of the house.

I ask Joel to fix me a hot ham and cheese with egg and grab my coffee. Lila saved me the seat at the very end of the bar.

"So, I had this weird dream last night." I tell her over our shared supper.

"Yeah, what about?" she asks, cutting into her potato.

"There was some woman drowning and a man in a devil mask, like the one that took me." I shivered, lowering my voice.. "And the woman spoke to me."

"Spoke to you?"

"'You know where I am, find me.' I have no idea who she was, but I do think I know where she is."

"Where? Is it somewhere around here?"

"Lover's Lookout, in a car submerged in the lake." I say

"Okay." Lila says.

"We should go look for her." I say.

"I don't think that's a good idea." Lila says, something in her eyes tells me she doesn't want to.

"Well, her family has been waiting all this time for answers. Let's give them that." I say, holding on to her wrist.

She shakes me off and says, "Fine."

I eat and my break is up before I know it. Lila leaves and I resume my shift. Nelson and Edna tipped me $100. Karol and her cronies tipped me nothing but Jesse left me a note and $20. The note read: "You look really cute in your uniform. See you Monday, xoxo". Asides from this, I see Ophelia crying on the phone. She must be talking to her husband.

Ophelia's daughter, Samantha, has been missing for a couple months. She's been frantic since she's been gone. She told me the news a couple nights ago. There was a new segment that covered her disappearance. She was going to class and was never seen again.

The next thing I know, my shift was over and I was in bed. That next morning, I leave for the woods early. Before leaving, I put on a halter bikini top under my hoodie.

"Where you going this early on a Sunday?" Mama asks as I lug my bag onto my back.

"I'm going for a walk, I'll be back before service, Mama. I love you." I kiss her on the forehead and head for Gorin Ridge.

Gorin Ridge is nicknamed Lover's Lookout. It's where couples go to watch the sunset and stargaze and…other things.. It's beautiful at night but it was pretty eerie in my dream.

I called Lila on the way there.

"Hey, meet me at Lover's Lookout?"

"Yeah, where are you?"

" I'm on Nebo Rd."

"I'll pick you up."

Gorin Ridge wasn't that far from Harlan Court. It was about a ten minute walk. Lila met me halfway there. I got into her car and we drove the rest of the way. The Ridge is a quaint camping ground. Well, used to be. Now it's a RV park and Lodge. A lot has changed in the past two years since I've been gone.

"Do you know who the drowning woman is?" Lila inquired as she pulled into the parking lot of the twin River RV Park and Lodge.

I take off my hoodie and keep on my jeans.

"You invited me for a swim? I should've brought my swimsuit." she joked.

"Not yet, but maybe there's some clues out here." We head down the big trail that's big enough for a car to fit through. There's cabins and parking spaces for RV's to either side of us. I look further down the trail and see an abandoned cabin off in the trees. That's totally not suspicious at all, considering how well-kept the rest of the park is. I walk past the "No campers beyond this point!" sign and open the door.

"Let's check something out first." I say as I get the door unlocked. Picking the lock, I finally hear it click.

When I open the door, the smell of old rain and soot hits me. I look around the cabin, it's old and worn down. The ceiling is dripping and the fireplace was recently lit. There's a coffee table, a couch, and a kitchen table. Looking to my left, I find a box filled with photos and a dragon claw necklace. They were photos of the girl from my dream. She is hugging someone that has been ripped out of the picture. But her big smile tells me that she's happy with whoever it is.

I peek into the bedroom and it's got fresh bed sheets and the closet is filled with clean clothes. On the top shelf of the closet, there's a manila folder that's about two inches thick. There's a journal on the nightstand.

Someone has been living here for a while. There are used dishes in the sink and coffee still in the coffee pot in the kitchen too. When I hold my hand next to the pot, it's still warm. I sprint out of the derelict cabin and almost run into Lila at the clearing.

"Lila! There's someone living here. They have photos of the girl I had a dream of." I say as I drag her with me through the cabin. Lila seems reluctant to go further into the cabin. I don't know why but she doesn't like this at all. She covers her mouth as she walks out the back door.

"Mia, you might want to take a look at this." she says with eyes wide. I look out the back door and see Lila standing there, frozen. Going out the back door, I go to the edge. There's the car from my dream. The woman was half flesh and half bone. We run back to Lila's car and Lila suggests we call the police. I call them anonymously so we don't get in trouble. That image will stay in my mind for as long as I live.

"Wait, I have to see something." I say before the police arrive. I sneak back into the cabin and take the manila folder and journal. I race back to Lila's car and we tear down the dirt road as quickly as we can.

Chapter Five: The News

"In later news tonight, partial skeletal remains have been found at the edge of Gorin Ridge. An anonymous tip was given to the police. Investigators are on the scene of the crime." said Jan Westin, the newscaster for EKYT. The camera switches over to the ridge, showing rescue divers towing a car out of the lake. The county coroner is on the scene with a gurney and a filled body bag. Jan comes back across the screen. "More information on this finding will come in later news."

"That's sad, isn't it?" sighs Mama as she takes a drink of her coffee. That woman loves her coffee, no matter what time of the day it is. "Yeah, I hope it's not one of my old classmates." Leona chimes in. In her class of 2015, three girls went missing right before graduation. Two of them were found alive in different states. "You don't think it's Claire, do you? They never found her."

"I don't know, but she was such a nice girl. Never caused trouble, never did wrong." Mama responds, cutting her eyes over at my sister. The word stung Leona like an angry bee. She then turns to me, dropping the scowl. "Baby girl, it's time for bed. You got school in the mornin'." I go to bed wondering what significance Claire is to Leona. I've never met her and she's never mentioned her. Maybe she's just an old friend. I ask Leona if she has any old yearbooks.

"Yeah from my senior year of high school, why?" Leona asks.

"I'm trying to see something. A man came in tonight and said he knew you." I lie.

Leona goes to her room and looks for the yearbook. She hands it to me and I begin flipping through it. I stop at the seniors and find the photo of the girl. Her name is Claire Chesterfield.

Chapter Six: House Fire

The sounds of distant sirens and the smell of smoke wake me. Getting out of bed, I stumble into my shoes. Running down the stairs, no one is in the house.

I walk out to the street and see that Mr. Elman's house is ablaze. Mama and Leona areoutside in their house robes and bonnets shivering from the cold.

"Lord have mercy, I hope James is alright!" Mama exclaims as the house billows black smoke into the dawn sky.

The EMTs arrive and administer oxygen to the frail old man as he coughs up black mucus. Firefighters work hard to diminish the blaze and then the unthinkable happens. The garage doors are blown off the hinges, a car tears down the street.

Mr. Elman and the EMTs are okay but Mr. Elman exclaims, "My car!

Someone stole my car! Somebody call the cops!"

"Go in and grab my phone, quick!" demands Mama. I run in and grab her phone off the dining room table. She's constantly forgetting her phone. She'd lose her head if it wasn't attached. I hand her the phone and she calls the Hollow Hill sheriff's department.

"Yes, my neighbor's car just got stolen on Harlan Court drive." Mama huffs to the operator, and explains the insanity we just witnessed. We live in the ghetto of Hollow Hill, full of subsidy apartments and run down shotgun houses. This is the second house fire to happen on our street in less than three months apparently. Due to the houses being so old, and the landlords being cheapskates, it was probably faulty wiring that caused both fires.

As the EMTs take Mr. Elman to the hospital, Leona and I shuffle back inside to get ready for school. She gets ready for her college classes and I get ready for my first day at Freeman Academy. It's my senior year and I'm just ready for school to be over with. I tie my box braids into a low messy bun and throw on my usual fit.

"The 90's called, they want the grunge girl look back." Leona jokes. She's right; I'm wearing a Nirvana t-shirt, a red flannel, ripped jeans and a pair of sneakers I probably should've thrown out years ago.

"You look like your daddy," Mama sighs. "That man loves 90's rock." Mama left Daddy after his relapse. I lived with him for almost three years before he started to drink again. He went to rehab and now he lives in Louisville. I'm going to visit him this weekend. Hopefully we can go to McQuixote's like we used to every weekend for coffee and to browse books. That's all I do when I don't have class is read.

"C'mon Mia! We're gonna be late!" yellsLeona as she walks out the door. I half trot down the stairs and give Mama a kiss before we leave. As we get in the car, the police pull in at Mr. Elman's. It's only one squad car but two policemen are talking to him. Three cars chase Mr. Elman's Cadillac DeVille down side streets and out of town.

"That's one way to start the day," Leona mumblesas she drives down Harlan Court. "Do you think it was arson or faulty wiring?"

"Faulty wiring, definitely. His landlord is too lazy to fix anything in that house." I say as I watch rows of shotgun houses roll past. "Why would you think it's arson?" I giggled.

"What if his landlord was tired of fixing the place up and decided to burn it down for insurance money?" she huffed. As I chewed it over, it made sense. The landlord never came when James complained about the outlets shorting out. It's probably just a bad case of the Mondays, nothing sinister

But as she pulled up to the academy to drop me off, a strong gut feeling that something was wrong suddenly overtook me.

Chapter Seven: The Green Light

I got to my first class of the day, English. Miss Anderson assigned the class to read *The Great Gatsby*. "Class, what does the green light at the end of the bay signify?" she inquires as she walks around the classroom.

I have the book in my hands reading ahead of the class. It was so good I couldn't put it down, plus I had to catch up to begin with.

"Mia? Can you tell us what it symbolizes?" Miss Anderson asks again as the class turns and stares at me.

"The green light symbolizes Gatsby's love for Daisy, and their unreachable future together." I say without even looking up from the book.

"Very good, Mia." she praises.

Karol and her little flunkies roll their eyes when they catch me glancing back at them.

"You're a dork." Karol giggled with her friends. If that's the best she's got, I'm not even gonna respond. That pisses her off more anyway.

Lila's seat is directly behind mine of course. She taps my shoulder while Miss Anderson moves on to the next assignment. "I want to slap that smug look off her face." she hisses under her breath before getting to what she really wants."Are you going to Atterly's party tomorrow night?" Jesse

Atterly, another boy in our grade, is having his annual Halloween Fest at his parents' mansion. Do his parents know? Doubt it. Is it on their dime? Always.

"Uh no. That's the last place I want to be. Besides, me and Leona are having a masked hotties marathon."

"C'mon girl, it'll be loads of fun. I'll bring the alcohol and you can bring the bud." Lila whispers.

Wrong again. The last time I had any bud in my possession, me and dad smoked all of it before it got anywhere else, and that was two years ago.

Still, I can't let Lila go alone, who knows what kinda trouble she'll get into without me. "Fine, I guess I'll have to tell her to wait up for me." Miss Anderson dismisses us, and I text my sister the change of plans. Jesse comes down the hall looking as handsome as ever.

"Hey girls! Y'all coming to the Halloween Fest tomorrow night?" he chimes as we walk toward him.

"I'm all in for tomorrow night. I gotta get my fake ID from Connor first so I can get the supplies." Lila replies, but he glosses right over her to check my response.

"You coming, Mia? I'd really love it if you came too."

"Yeah, sure thing babes." I feel my cheeks flush as at the last word. It just slipped right out like my brain-to-mouth filter shut off at the worst time ever.

"Damn, get a room already you two!" Lila snaps, breaking me from Jesse's gaze.

"I'll see you in chem, uh, dude." I stutter as we walk past him.

"Really, dude? Is that the best you can do?" Lila jabs, her tone unusually short and impatient.

"I like him, okay? He may be with Karol but he's always had a thing for me." I insist as I stuff my English books in my bag.

"Yeah, I can tell by the way he stares at you from Mr. McAfee's class." Lila says with an eye roll.

Jesse is one of the top students in Mr. McAfee's class. Not only is he hot, he's smart too. Lila's favorite subject is chemistry, but she likes the professor more than she does the class itself.

From what Lila tells me, Mr. McAfee is young and charming. He got his bachelor's in organic chemistry then worked for a pharmaceutical company before he started teaching. His looks keep all the girls' attention in class; he's got black hair, green eyes, and he's well over six feet. He's got a sleeper build, but you can see his muscles under his thin button-ups.

I look at Lila and she's staring him down. She smiles at him when he looks at her. He winks and smirks back. I have to nudge her a million times just to get her attention.

"Girl, did I tell you what happened this morning?" I ask Lila, trying to bring her back down out of the clouds.

"Huh? What?"turning sideways in her chair, she finally focuses. I give her the rundown of the drama I watched unfold across the street, and that seems to shock her back to reality. .

"That's insane and so random."

"Yeah. I don't know if the cops caught them either. Leona believes the house was arson and the landlord is responsible."

"I honestly believe it. The ones I know are so sketchy."

"Anyway, I think that the ghost I communicated with is a missing person."

"Really?"

"Yeah, we should go to the library and see what we can find."

"Alright. Sounds like a plan." Lila says.

Chapter Eight: The Archives

After school lets out, Lila and I stop downtown at the Hollow Hill Public Library. It is bustling with older people using the computers and younger people perusing the shelves. We ask the archivist if we can access newspapers from the early 2010's. She opens a large book that has newspaper clippings ranging from 2010 to 2019. We thank her and start our search.

"She had black hair and blue eyes. She would've been at least our age when she disappeared." I say as I'm scanning through missing persons sections. There are several young women that have gone missing in the past. They started disappearing in the nineties. When Dad and Mama were our age.

"Here she is! Her name was Claire Chesterfield. She went missing from a house party. She looks exactly the same as she did when she was in my dream." I tell Lila. "I don't know how I'm going to tell Leona that I found her friend in the river."

"Leona knew her?"

"Yeah, they worked together at Hodge's." I add. Hodge's is a popular bar and restaurant on the east side of town.

"How did a ghost come to you? Are you doing seances in your spare time?" Lila jokes as she stares at the photo.

"No, but she really did come to me asking for help." I say, thinking back to the night before. "We need to do some more research on Claire and that cabin to see what leads we have, okay?" I close the folder and put it on the return cart. "We need to go through the stuff I found"

"Stuff you found? We're not CSI and that's stealing!" she hisses, looking over her shoulder to see if anyone heard her.

"I know it's a bad idea but it wouldn't hurt to look. Maybe we can find something that will help."

"Alright, Detective Mia."
We go to the computer lab before leaving and look for any updates on the body we found at Lover's Lookout online. They found a dragon claw circlet around her arm. The article also said that the forensics team will be looking at dental records to make a match.

I see Mr. Elman's Cadillac in the grocery store parking lot on our way home. I go over to investigate closer and see there's a familiar devil mask in the passenger seat. I gasp and step back. *Oh no, he's back.* I feel my throat close up and it's hard for me to breathe. I'm about to have a panic attack.

Chapter Nine: Hallow's Eve

Tonight is Jesse's Halloween Fest, and almost everyone from school will be there. There will be alcohol, drugs, and who knows what else will go on. Maybe we'll slow dance tonight. I stuff my mask and costume into my backpack and head downstairs.

"Mia! Get your behind down here! Lila's here to take y'all to that party." Mama calls upstairs. Lila is dressed in her best "final girl" garb. Ripped jeans, a torn bloody t-shirt and combat boots. Mama kisses me on the forehead as we leave. "Don't be late, girl! I'll have your behind if you are!" she hollers out the door.

When we get in Lila's car, she pulls out her backpack. It's filled with alcohol and condoms. "Ya girl is gettin' laid tonight!" she chuckles. "Maybe you and Jesse will have a good night too." she tosses a rubber at me jokingly.

My reflexes kick in and I swat it into the floorboard. "I don't think so, he's still with Karol."

"They aren't going to stay together forever, love. It'll hit the fan when he finds out she's been cheating on him with his best friend, Zach."

"Of course she would cheat on him, fucking witch." I hissed.

"I found out when I saw Karol sucking face with Zach." Lila says.
We get to his house on the other side of town in Knocknee Hills. It's a gated community with rows of large mansions and manicured lawns. When we pull in, there are people at the front door waiting to get in. Lila's clunker stands out from the rest. Everyone else is driving a Mercedes or better.

"Hey girls!" Jesse yells and waves us through the line .
We cut through the crowd and walk into the mansion. It's gorgeous; there's a chandelier in the foyer

and a large bouquet of hydrangeas on a table as you walk in.

Jesse is dressed in a patient zero zombie costume that's tattered and bloody. I wonder what his girlfriend is wearing. Probably dressed like the bimbo in those apocalypse movies.

Speak of the devil. "Hey babe, you wanna go upstairs?" Karol slurs, hanging on him like a dirty rag. She reeks of alcohol and cigarettes.

"No, you reek. Go by yourself. I want to entertain my guests." he winks at me. He takes my hand and we go to the kitchen.

"What would you like to drink?" he starts to make his own mixed drink. I choose to stay non alcoholic and grab a soda from the cooler.

"Playing it safe, are we?" he jokes.

"Yeah, I should in case Lila gets too wild." I say as I take another sip. I look in the living room and I see her in the corner talking to a man wearing a wooden mask with goat horns.

"Who is that talking to Lila?" I pull him over and point to them. He knows everyone in this little town either through school or his parents businesses, so his answer scares me.

"I don't know. Maybe we should go over there and whisk her away." Concerned, we both head in Lila's direction.

"Hey, Lila!" I wave at her. Her eyes are low and she's moving sluggishly. She half waves and goes back to ogling at the goat horns.

*****

As I'm sitting there, Lila and I hear a large commotion coming from upstairs. It was Jesse throwing a vase at Zach's head. He runs down the stairs with his pants half done; Karol is behind him in only a bedsheet.

"What the fuck, Karol?! You're cheating on me with Zach??" Jesse screamed, looking for something to throw at Zach.

"Babe, it's not what it looks like." she whimpers.

"The hell it is! You will never see me again, you hear me?!?" he hissed.

I nudge Lila and smile as we watched the drama unfold. Jesse grabbed Zach by the hair and threw him out of the front door.

Everyone that was paying attention, gave him a round of applause. He took off his shoes and said, "The party will go on! No woman is going to stop this party!" he goes over to the stereo and turns it up.

I looked around to see if goat horns was still around. He is, but he's shaking with anger. He slams his drink down on the piano and storms off.

"Lila, I need you to go to the car now. You've had enough to drink."

"Yes ma'am" she slurs.

Helping her up, I notice goat horns is in the vicinity of the front door. I guide past him and take her down the steps. She's dragging her feet and it's hard to keep a grasp on her. I hoist her up by the arms and put her in the car. She gives me the keys and I lock the doors. I go back in and grab my backpack. The guy in the goat horns trots down the steps and begins walking down the sidewalk. He stops at Lila's car and tries to get in. He reaches into his pocket and jimmies the door open. He speeds off and takes Lila God knows where.

Chapter Ten: Gone

Jesse sits on the stoop with me as I call the police. I'm shaking and I can hardly breathe. The operator tells me that it has to be two days before they can do anything.

"Two days?! She could be dead by then!" I shout into the phone.

I hang up and shove it in my bag. I hang my head and begin to sob. Jesse rubs my back and hugs me. He kisses me on the temple and rocks me side to side. The comfort soothes me a little.

"Give me your phone and I'll call your sister," he says.

I grab my phone out of the bag and hand it to him. He goes through my contacts and calls Leona. He paces the steps as he's making the call. A few minutes felt like an eternity as she finally pulled up. Jesse gives me a hug and I walk down the steps. Getting in, Leona gives me a look of worry. Her eyes are filled with a familiar sadness. Like she's been through this before.

"Any idea where she could be?" Leona asks.

"No."

"Hopefully they find her soon."

"Yeah I hope so."

The rest of the ride was quiet. Mama is standing at the edge of the steps. She's in her house robe and bonnet. Her brow is wrinkled and she's clutching the hem of her robe.

"Are you alright, baby?" she asks as I get out of the car.

"I'm as okay as I can be." I say, storming past her.

Going up to my room, I get in bed. I curl up and hold my pillow. I begin to sob again until I fall asleep. Then the nightmares begin.

I see myself running from a bird's eye view. Lila is with me and she falls behind. A blackness covers her. The Devil Mask killer grabs her by the hair and slices her throat. Throwing her to the ground, he comes after me next. His voice is distorted as he says, "Come here, little rabbit!". Running with nowhere to go, I make it to the clearing. I dive into the water and swim to the other side. Going against the current, I see him dive after me. Making it to the other side, I see that the water is still. No one is in the water. Turning around, he grabs me by the throat. As he plunges me into the water, I wake up.

In a cold sweat, I get out of bed and sit at my desk. My laptop pings with a notification. I open it and it's a video. It's Lila, she's being dragged by goat horns. She has a black bag over her head and he drags her up the steps. I don't know who sent this. It's from an email I don't recognize.

Chapter Eleven: Missing

It's Tuesday and Lila still hasn't shown up to school. She hasn't answered my calls or texts either. *She always messages me.*

Miss Anderson looks at me with concern as she passes out quizzes from last week. "Mia, are you okay?"

"Yeah, I'm fine. It's just my head hurts." It wasn't a lie, my whole skull was throbbing from a stress headache. It felt like someone hit me in the forehead with an ice pick.

"Go to the nurse." She hands me a hall pass and pats my shoulder.

I gather my things and trudge down the hall. The hall lights are so bright it hurts my eyes. I feel like throwing up.

When I look down the hallway towards the nurse's office, I see three policemen. One of them is wearing a suit. He's got grayish brown hair, a beard, and a beer gut.

I make it to the nurse's office and I explain that I have a migraine. She gives me some Excedrin and a cool rag to put on my forehead. I lay on the bed in the back of her office and I close my eyes.

I can hear the conversation that's going on in the next room; the officers aren't exactly whispering.

"Can you tell me where you were the night Atkins went missing?"

"I was at home. I never talked to her that night." says a voice I don't recognize.

"Do you know of anyone who did?"

"Yeah. Her name is Mia Audley. She's in Miss Anderson's room right now."

I roll off of the bed and walk to the front of the office. The nurse stepped out for lunch and I was the only one left in here. The cops are going towards Miss Anderson's room now, looking for me. I feel my heart drop and I feel a flutter in my stomach. *How in the hell did Lila go missing?* I thought to myself. What do I tell the police?

I slink back down the hall towards Miss Anderson's room and find them at the door with my teacher.

She points behind them to indicate my approach, and they turn to greet me. "Alright, thank you." said the portly detective.

"Mia Audley?" he addresses me.

"Yes, sir. What happened?"

"Lila Atkins has gone missing and we'd like to know if you talked to her Saturday night."

"The last time I saw her was at Jesse Atterly's party. She was supposed to ride with me, but her and the car were gone." I say. But

I don't tell them she was talking to a man at the party.

"Okay, here's my information in case you remember anything else." the detective hands me a card that reads:

Detective John Tremble # 555-8035

"Alright, thanks. " I slip his card into my pocket. Detective Tremble and the other two policemen hang around for a while longer. Classes droned on. All I could think about was the stuff I grabbed from that cabin. After school I'm going to go to Witch's Brew. It's a coffee shop on the corner of town.

The only plus to today was that Jesse gave me his number.

I get out of school and Leona picks me up. I told her that the police came and talked to me about Lila.

"What? She's missing?"

"Yeah, she must have disappeared the night of the party." I say, thinking about where I put all the evidence. It must be in my other bag in my closet.

"You ain't thinking about finding her yourself are you?" Leona asks, knowing I'm going to.

"Well, the police are doing their thing, let me do mine." I say, putting my book back in my bag.

We pull up to the house and I get out. Leona has to get to work. I get into the house and find mama asleep on the couch. I find a manila envelope addressed to my name on the coffee table. I open it and I can't believe what I'm seeing. It's a photo of me getting out of the taxi my first day back. In red, it says, "Welcome Home, Mia". I feel wrong. I feel violated. I'm being watched. The photo was taken from across the street. Mama wakes up and I feel the sudden urge to leave.

"Hey mama, I'm going for a walk." I told her. I didn't tell her that Lila had gone missing. I go to the local coffee shop, Witch's Brew, and have a look at the stuff I got from the cabin. I grab my phone. I rummage through my bag and find Jesse's number. I call him:

"Hello, is this Jesse Atterly?"

"Yes, who is this?"

"It's Mia from chem."

"Hey, honey! What's up?"

"I think Lila is missing."

"Oh no, why do you say that?"

"She hasn't called or texted me since last night and I have her car keys. The police came to school and questioned me."

"That's not a good sign, where are you?"

"I'm at witch's brew. Trying to plan my next move."

"I'll be right there."

I wait for ten minutes and he pulls in. The door's bell rings overhead and he's absolutely stunning.

"Hey. What was her last location? She has an iPhone, right?"

"No but she has snapchat. I can check her location from there."

I check her bitmoji on snapchat and it says she's at Gorin Ridge. I think back to the cabin and know exactly where to look. But I have a bad feeling about the whole situation.

I open the manila folder and find a lot of photos of Lila in various locations. I mean *a lot*. There are notes on the photos that say, "Mia Audley's best friend?" Then in red marker there's an A written on her forehead and it says "WHORE" in all caps. I feel my stomach drop. That cabin is where Devil Mask lives. "She's at Lover's Lookout. We need to get to her immediately." I say while I put my phone and manila folder in my bag. This is bad, really bad.

"Don't you think we should call the police?" he said with his eyes sparkling with concern.

"I don't want to get the police involved yet, they're already up to their gills with the body they found." I said

"What if the body they found and Lila going missing are connected somehow?" Jesse asked.

"Like a serial kidnapper?"

"No, worse. A serial killer."

The word *killer* stuck in my mind. What if Lila is already dead? What if the killer already disposed of her body? What's his motive?

"I need to go to Lover's Lookout to find Lila and bring her home. I can't let my best friend get killed."

"Okay, but we should really call the police."

My phone rang, it's Leona.

"Girl, do you know when you'll be home? Mama's worried about you."

"Yeah I'll be there in an hour. I'm having coffee with a friend of mine."

"Well, that friend of yours best be cute."

"Oh trust me he is."

"Okay, well, I'll call you later. Don't be late coming home."

As I hang up, Jesse gives me a coy look. "You think I'm cute?"

"Yes, I've always thought you were." I say, looking into those beautiful hazel eyes.

"Now, would you like to help me find Lila?" I ask her, hoping he'd say yes.

"Yes, I'll help you. But on one condition."

"What's the one condition?"

"After this is all over, we go on a date."

"I can go for that." I say, I feel like I'm over the moon.

We get into the car and go to Twin Rivers RV Lodge. The parking lot is empty. I have a bad feeling about this. Before I get out of the car, I tell Jesse the truth.

"You know how I was gone for almost two years?" I ask, looking into his eyes.

"Yeah, you were with your dad, right?" he says, smiling at me.

"No, I was at Westbrook Psychiatric Hospital." I say, digging half crescents into my palms

"Why were you there?" he asks, looking at me with concern.

"I was kidnapped and almost killed by the Devil Mask killer. My mom thought I was lying and needed a psych eval." I say, my eyes stinging with tears.

"Look at what he did to me." I say, lifting my shirt. My scars are welted and pink.

"What did he do to you?" he asks with horror.

"He beat me with a whip. He planned to kill me." I say, fully crying now.

I start to sob and I get out of the car. I hate it when people see me cry. Dr. Edmundson was wrong, I'm not ready for the world. Jesse gets out of the car and hugs me. He kisses me on the forehead, "It'll be alright, my love. I'm here for you." I return the embrace and wipe my eyes. "Lila got kidnapped because of me. He's trying to get revenge." I say, I need to be strong for Lila and Jesse.

"I think I found something, Mia." Jesse says as he holds up Lila's backpack. I check the bag and there's a broken vodka bottle in the bottom. I cut my hand. The alcohol got into the gash on my palm, sending a searing pain through my arm.

"Shit! That hurts."

"Are you okay?" he says, grabbing my hand.

The gash is deep, blood is saturating the ground below.

"Yeah, I'll be okay."

He goes to his car and grabs gauze from his trunk.

"Here, wrap this around it." he says as he hands it to me. I wrap my hand as tightly as possible. I tell Jesse to stay with the car in case of a quick getaway.

I head down the trail and go to the derelict cabin.

I sneak towards the backdoor and spot him in the window. His back is turned and he appears to be on the phone. I go to the bedroom window and see Lila. She's still alive, thank God. But she's blindfolded and her wrists are tied together. I try to open the bedroom window and it's nailed shut. To no avail, I try the next window. It's the one to the bathroom in the bedroom. It's unlocked and I crawl through the low window.

"Lila, I'm here to get you out." I whisper.

"No, Mia, he'll kill you too." she hissed back

"Let me figure something out." I say weighing my options. I hear heavy footsteps coming down the hallway, I hide in the closet near the bed.

"Was someone talking to you in here??" the man said. His voice was low and sweet, he didn't sound angry.

"No, there's no one here." Lila said as her head turned towards the bathroom. He was wearing that mask again. The wood is starting to crack around the edges of the mouth. He took her blindfold off and grabbed her by the chin.

"Why do the pretty ones always die in such horrible ways? You will be my Black Dahlia." the man sighed. He took her and threw her over his shoulder. He walks out of the room. I look out the window and he's putting her in his trunk. He parked Mr. Elman's car on the other side of the cabin. I run to the front door and see Jesse's car. I bolt out the door and make it to Jesse's car.

"He's taking Lila somewhere else. I don't know where but I'm sure we don't have much time."

Chapter Twelve Lila's Apartment

Jesse takes me to Lila's apartment and I find that it's unlocked. I sneak in and go to her bedroom. I found a purple journal. I read the first few pages and it was a description of her first day living here. I found something strange about it though. She never mentioned a man named Jake. Jake was apparently her next door neighbor but I've never seen anyone. She talks about how strange this guy is and how he never speaks. He just stares at her every time he's outside.

I take the journal with me and I feel guilty for going through her personal things. I find her phone and take it as well. Now it's time to go through all the evidence. Me and Jesse go back to my house and we start to look through everything. We find a journal entry in Lila's journal that suggests

Connor Janes could possibly be a suspect:

I'm scared for my life. I owe Connor money and he said he'd kill me if I didn't give him the money by Friday. Money has been tight lately with the cost of living here and saving for college. I never should've borrowed that money from him. He's been passing by my house like clockwork. He even left a note on my front door telling me to pay up or else. What should I do?? I can't call the police. I'd definitely be dead if I called them.

I leave Lila's apartment and find her neighbor sitting outside. He asks, "Is Lila okay? She hasn't been home for a few days."

"I don't know. I just came by to get my phone." I lie and leave. The man stares me down as I get in the car to leave. I see what Lila means by that guy gives her the creeps.

"We need to talk to Connor." I say, going through the journal.

"Connor Janes, the druggie?" he says

"He's not a druggie, he just deals with them." I say, wondering why Lila would borrow money from a drug dealer.

"Whatever you say. But how are we going to get in contact with him?" he asks, turning into Witch's Brew's parking lot. I see a police cruiser in the parking lot as we pull in. Detective Tremble is talking to the barista as we walk in. Detective Tremble asked me if I heard or saw anything. I tell him no. He looks at me as if I'm a suspect then leaves.

The barista, Sandra, asks for our order.

"I'll have a large coffee. Black." I say

"I'll take a hazelnut macchiato." said Jesse

We found a table in the back of the cafe to look over the evidence I found. I pull out Lila's phone and look at the photos. I find a picture of Mr. McAfee and Lila. They're smiling cheek to cheek in the photo.

We grab our order and head back to the table. I tell Jesse what I found in her journal.

"So Connor could be a suspect?"

"Yeah. Lila owed him money and she vanished soon after."

"I don't think he would do anything to hurt her."

"Well, we still need to talk to him."

"Yeah, we'll have to talk to him after I come back from my trip with my dad."

"Okay."

He looks at me in the eyes and grabs my hand. I feel my cheeks flush and I feel sort of embarrassed. I smile and kiss his hand. We leave the cafe and he drops me off at home.

Chapter Thirteen: Home

"Mia! Dad's here to pick you up!" Leona yelled up the stairs.

"I'm still packing!" I yelled back "Tell him to come to my room!"

Dad comes up the stairs and he looks great. His blue eyes aren't bloodshot anymore. They look like pools of scandinavian ice. His black hair and beard are peppered with gray. He's wearing a ramones shirt, a black flannel, and a pair of levis.

"Hey girl, it's time to hit the road."

"I know, I'm almost ready."

"What's that?" he asks, pointing toward the dragon claw necklace.

"Oh, it's from a friend of mine." I say, knowing it's a lie.

"It looks familiar." he says

"How?" I ask him incredulously

"A friend of a friend had one exactly like that. His girlfriend had a circlet that went around her arm. She went missing a few years back."

My eyes widen and I get a pang of fear in my gut.

"You okay, Mia? You look like you've seen a ghost."

"Dad, we need to talk in the car."

"Okay, are you all set then?"

"Yup." I say as I grab my phone and charger off the nightstand

"So, Mia, what were you going to talk to me about?" Dad asks, looking over at me.

I go over the missing persons case, how she communicated with me, and how there's a possible serial killer on the loose. He looks at me, stunned.

"Is it the same guy that-"

"Yeah."

"Do you think that guy killed the girl?"

"Yeah, I found her and her car at Lover's Lookout near his cabin."

"He wasn't there, was he?"

"No. But I noticed that she had a circlet around her arm. It was a dragon claw holding a moonstone." I say looking down at the pendant.

"Who gave you that necklace?" Dad asks with a hardened tone.

"I found it at the Lookout."

"I think I know who that pendant belongs to." Dad says

He goes to Mr. Elman's old house and looks dismayed.

"What happened to Mrs. McAfee's house?" Dad asks me.

"Mrs. McAfee? The only person I knew that lived here was Mr. Elman."

"Well, that pendant belonged to her son. He almost died a few years ago from a drug overdose. He was a strange fella, but he was misunderstood." Dad said looking back at the burnt house.

"Isn't Mr. McAfee's mom sick?"

"No, Mrs. McAfee died mysteriously a few years ago. No one ever knew what happened to her. Didn't find her either." Dad said

I had a horrible feeling in my stomach. I felt compelled to go into the basement of that burnt down apartment.

"Dad, I'll be right back."

I go to the garage of the house. I didn't find anything. But I smell a faint tinge of desiccated flesh. We go to the basement and find the door is charred. I open it and find a table with charred human remains. This is where the fire started. The gas can and lighter were lying on the table. There are blades and other weapons hanging on the wall.

  I think I found Mrs. McAfee. But there's no way that's her. Mr. McAfee said she was in the hospital. But from the way the last couple days have gone, I wouldn't be surprised if she was actually dead. I go through the rest of the room and I find another journal. It's like the one from the cabin. It's gotta belong to Devil Mask. It's partially burnt but the pages are still legible. I take it with me and I leave.

"Find anything interesting?" Dad asks

"Yeah, I found charred remains." I say

"Charred remains? It might be Mrs. McAfee. I'm surprised they didn't look when they investigated the fire."

"They haven't done an investigation yet. Mr. Elman is still in the hospital."

"Oh."

We leave the house and hit the road. When we get on the exit for Louisville, I drift off in the passenger seat and dreamt of Claire again. This time she was alive. A man gives her a gift box, she opens it and it's the circlet. Its silver shined and the moonstone twinkled. The man leaned down and kissed her.
"Happy birthday, my love." said the man.
"Thank you, honey. I love it." said Claire
Then the dream goes to them having an argument.

"I told you I wasn't cheating! Stop believing what other people say!" Claire exclaimed.

The man yells something that's unintelligible and slaps her. He then proceeds to wail on her relentlessly.

"Honey, I'm sorry I don't mean to hurt you but you know what happens when you lie to me." Then he keeps hitting her.

"Stop, please! I'm sorry!" Claire pleads over and over.

I feel a nudge and it's dad. I woke up in a panic.

"Hey, we're here."

"Okay, I'll be there in a second." I say, eyes wide.

I tried to decipher what that dream meant. She was in an abusive relationship and she had no way out. She was murdered.

I check my phone for any updates on Claire Chesterfield. A family member positively identified her by a birthmark. I would've hated to see the sadness in their faces. I told dad the news.

"Hey dad, the girl they found was actually Claire Chesterfield. The woman from my dream."

"Well I be damned."

"I knew it was her. See, I told you that she was communicating with me."

"It's just weird. I mean, why did she communicate with you?"

"I don't know but I think she was murdered by her fiance."

"Why do you think so?"

"Because I just had another dream of her and she was being abused. I think I saw her last moments."

"Whoa."

Chapter Fourteen: Recovery Party

"This party is going to be amazing, Dad." I say

"Yeah, I'm excited to see all my friends from years ago. I wish Claire could've been there. Too bad that happened to her." Dad said with sorrow in his eyes.

I hope she gets the justice she deserves. What happened to her is absolutely horrid. The police found her upper torso in the front seat and her lower half in trash bags in the trunk. The man dismembered her.

Someone stuck the car in reverse and put a brick on the gas.

"Who will be there, Dad?" I ask. I never met his friends before.

"Emil, Jack, Evelyn just to name a few." he says

"We need to find costumes for tonight. It's Halloween themed."

I look at dad and do an eye roll.

"C'mon it'll be fun" Dad teased "We'll go to the old halloween shop we used to go to."

"Okay, what should I wear?"

Dad looks at me up and down and says, "Maybe a hannya, you love Japanese mythos."

I grin and agree with him. Hannyas are female demons in Japanese mythology. They are a sign of good luck. They have really cool masks at Caufield's. They also have really cool costumes.

We got to his party at a small house in Portland. Portland is a neighborhood in Louisville. There were a lot of people. Dad walks in and they all yell, "Congratulations!"

Dad is greeted by a woman wearing a red dress with a nurse's cap. I'm guessing her name is Evelyn. Dad introduces us and then he introduces me to Emil. Emil is wearing a rabbit mask.

"Hello, my name is Emil." he says with cadence.

"Hi, my name is Mia. Nice to meet you." I say. His voice is deep but his tone is sweet. He seems like a nice guy.

"What's up?" I say, not knowing how to start the conversation.

"Oh nothing much, just hoping my brother doesn't ruin your dad's party."

"Your brother?"

Then I see Mr. McAfee in the corner wearing a goat mask. I feel my stomach drop and my hands start to shake. I excuse myself and find the bathroom. I take my anxiety medicine and take a second to breathe. *He can't be the man that kidnapped Lila. She's a student of his. That would be immoral and wrong. Why would he?* I think to myself. I splash cold water on my face and walk out of the bathroom. Emil is standing at the food table, talking to Mr. McAfee. I walk over and Emil greets me with a smile.

"Everything okay?" he says, looking at me with concern.

"Yeah, I'm fine. It's just nerves." I say, looking past him at Mr. McAfee. They look identical. The only difference is that Mr. McAfee has a scar on his right palm and on his eyebrow. That's where the man cut his hand when he kidnapped me. The man wore sunglasses and a mask because it was during covid season. I'm afraid this is the same man.

"Hello, Mia. This is one of my students, Emil. She's a bright young lady." he slurs. He's been drinking heavily. His eyes are starting to swim and he's leaning on the table. The table started to shift and he almost fell.

"It's truly sad what happened to Lila. I hope they find her soon." Emil says. His cadence left and his voice hardened when he said it. His eyes were filled with genuine worry and concern when he spoke of Lila. Mr. McAfee looks at his brother and laughs. "You sad sap, she's fine. I saw her yesterday, she's with her boyfriend."

"She doesn't have a boyfriend. She's been single for a long time." I say, thinking back to the night we went to Jesse's party. That man she was talking to seemed too old to be her boyfriend. I guess I don't know that much about Lila. A lot can happen in two years.

Chapter Fifteen: The Body

Claire's body was found almost three weeks ago. They made a positive ID by a family member. She had a distinct birthmark on her left shoulder. Dental records were also a match.

"I believe Claire was murdered by someone she knew," said Detective Tremble.

"What makes you say that?" asked the medical examiner

"She didn't have any defensive wounds." he said

"Well, whoever did this used lye and poured it onto her body." the medical examiner said. She unveiled Claire's body and there were chemical burns on her face, legs and arms. The lye melted the soft tissue and cartilage off of her face. You could see her jaw and the hole where her nose would've been. "I hope you catch the person that did this to her." the medical examiner said.

Detective Tremble turns to leave and says, "I will, that's a promise."

Chapter Sixteen: Let's Talk

Dad dropped me off at Mom's and I went to my room. There is a cold draft and I look to find the window was open. It was closed before I left. My room doesn't look tampered with but I check my closet and there's Lila's shirt.

It was the shirt she wore the night she disappeared. It had real blood mixed with the fake. A note was pinned to the collar. It read: "She's never coming home. She's mine!" I hold onto the shirt and think about what's happened to her. I need to get rid of this shirt before I become a suspect. Detective Tremble is already suspicious of me.

I throw the shirt in my bag but keep the note in the journal I took from the cabin. I take the evidence with me to Witch's brew. I call Jesse.

"Hey Jesse, can you meet me at Witch's Brew?"

"Yeah, what's up?"

"I just got a message from her kidnapper."

"What?"

"I walk into my room to find my window open. I look in my closet and find her shirt."

"Seriously? That's creepy."

"Yeah. We need to find her soon."

After I got off the phone, I ordered a chocolate chip muffin and a cup of black coffee. While I wait for Jesse, Detective Tremble comes in and orders a coffee. He notices that I'm sitting by the window. He comes over to talk to me.

"Hello, Mia. Why do you come here so often?"

"They have really good coffee and I was hoping I would see Lila working." I say, knowing this wasn't a lie.

"They mentioned she worked here. Has she turned up?"

"No, I'm really worried about my friend, detective."

"I understand. We're still looking for her."

Jesse comes through the door and sees him talking to me. He turns around and orders a coffee. He comes to the table and Detective Tremble leaves.

"What was that about?" he asks, watching him leave.

"He was just coming over to make conversation I guess." I say

"So, how are we going to contact Connor?" he asks, taking a sip of his coffee.

"I got Lila's phone. I thought it was weird that she would leave without it." I say, going through her contacts. I found Connor's address and number. I give Jesse the address and we head to Connor's house.

We pull up to a shotgun house that's got graffiti all over it. I knock on the door and a man answers. He's about six feet, brown hair and brown eyes.

"Connor?"

"Yeah, that's me. What's up?"

"I was wondering if you've seen Lila."

"I haven't seen her since Halloween. She was acting all weird though."

"Weird, how?" I asked

"She acted like someone was watching her." he replied

"Like someone was in the car waiting on her?" I grilled, there's no way someone was in the car with her that night. She was alone when she came and got me.

"Yeah. I saw a man sitting in the driver's seat of her car." he clarified.

"When did she come by?" I inquired. She didn't come by the house til 7.

"She came by at around 6. She was getting her fake ID to get alcohol." he answered.

"Ah, okay. She mentioned she owed you money. How much did she owe?" I ask

"Wouldn't you like to know," he retorted, "That cunt owes me over three grand." he continued.

From the way he's talking about her, he doesn't like her that much. I need to get more information but I can tell he's getting very irritated. I tell him goodbye and we leave.

"Do you think he's telling the truth?" Jesse asks, starting the car.

"Yeah, but my question is, why did she borrow so much?"

Chapter Seventeen: The Cabin of Horrors

Me and Jesse want to figure out who that man is. We're going to search his cabin and see what we can find. "What do you think we'll find?" I inquire as we're walking toward the cabin.

"I don't know, I'm honestly afraid to find out." Jesse shuddered.

We get to the cabin and find it's locked. I grab a couple bobby pins out of my hair and pick the lock. Once inside, there's an awful smell. It smells like rotten molasses.

We open the door to the bedroom and search the closet and nightstands. We find a manila folder, a journal, and an unmarked photo album. I also find Lila's boots in the top right corner of the closet. Once I grab the boots, a small box falls off the shelf.

It's a box of women's fingernails. They're all different shades of red, black, and pink. I feel sick to my stomach.

I opened the manila folder first.

My mouth is agape, "Jesse, you might want to look at this."

He hands me the manila folder and it has photos of Lila from junior year at various locations. Witch's Brew, Kroger, the library. This man has been stalking her for almost three years.

"The journal is even worse." I surmised

I open up the journal and the first entry reads:

2/14/2018

I WANT THE WORLD TO HAVE PURE WOMEN. WOMEN THAT HAVE NEVER LIED. WOMEN THAT HAVE NEVER CHEATED. I WANT THE WOMEN OF THE WORLD TO BE LIKE MOTHER. SHE WAS NEVER CROSS WITH ME UNTIL I STARTED TALKING TO THOSE HARLOTS AT SCHOOL. CLAIRE WAS SUCH A GOOD GIRL UNTIL SHE CHEATED ON ME! SHE NEVER SHOULD HAVE. SHE'S GOING TO PAY FOR MAKING ME A FOOL! I'M GOING TO KILL THAT WHORE!"

"So, this is the guy that killed Claire?" Jesse asks

"Yeah, in my dream he was very abusive towards her." I whispered

"Did she actually cheat on him?" Jesse inquired

"I don't think so, she was pleading for her life in my dream." I say, looking through the journal.

"Hey, do you remember Sam?"

"Yeah, didn't she transfer to another school?"

"No, he killed her for interrupting his talk with Lila."

"What? No way."

Another journal entry read:

10/31/2023

I DIDN'T MEAN TO KILL HER, BUT I HAD NO CHOICE. NO ONE GETS IN BETWEEN ME AND MY IT GIRL. SHE WASN'T A FRIEND TO HER ANYWAYS. SAM WAS A NICE GIRL UNTIL SHE INTERRUPTED MY TALK WITH LILA. LILA IS MY TYPE OF GIRL.

TALL, SMART, HAS THE CURVES OF ANY GROWN WOMAN. SHE IS HOT AND SHE IS MINE! TONIGHT I'LL HAVE HER IN MY ARMS. ALIVE OR DEAD.

TOO BAD I HAVE TESTS TO GRADE. NO ONE IN THAT CLASS UNDERSTANDS COVALENT BONDS LIKE LILA. SHE'S A GREAT STUDENT AND WILL MAKE THE PERFECT VICTIM.

I TOOK SAM'S BODY AND LAID IT ON THE SLAB IN THE BACK OF MY VAN. I START TAKING HER APART PIECE BY GRUELING PIECE. THIS IS GOING TO TAKE A WHILE. I USED A NEW SUBSTANCE THIS TIME TO DISSOLVE THE BODY. I USED HYDROCHLORIC ACID AND HER BODY WILL BE A PILE OF GOOP BY SUNDAY.

"This is so fucked up. Why kill her?" I say, looking at other pages. There are multiple pages about Lila and how she's the perfect victim.

"Probably for fun, honestly." Jesse shudders

I look at the photos and they're all marked with red ink. The words whore and harlot jump off the pages.

"Is this because she told him she didn't want him?" Jesse says to me.

"What do you mean 'didn't want him'?" I say with air quotes

"Before you came back from Westbrook, he asked Lila out," he says

"It was before spring break and he asked her to go with him to Tennessee." he continues

"Not only is he a killer, he's a damn pedo." I say with disgust.

Before I can say another word, I hear a car pull into the parking lot.

"Mia, we got to go now!" Jesse says

It was Detective Tremble and a couple police officers. We took the journal and ran toward the back door. We left before the door fully opened.

Chapter Eighteen: Evidence

Detective Tremble couldn't get over the awful smell of rotten molasses.

"There's a body here. We need to find it."

The closer Tremble got, the worse the smell became. He got to the cellar out back and found a woman's body suspended upside down like livestock. Her body was covered in deep gashes that had started to swell due to how long she'd been there. There was a wall full of weapons of torture. Then he heard a muffled scream in the corner. It was Lila Atkins. She was handcuffed to one of the beams. She was naked and covered in filth. The green eyed man wanted to leave her for dead.

Detective Tremble and the policemen take Lila to the station for questioning.

"So, Miss Atkins, how long were you captive for?"

"Four days, sir."

"Who did this to you?"

"Mr. McAfee, sir."

"The chemistry teacher?"

"Yes, sir, he drugged me and put me in the trunk of his car."

"How'd you know it was Mr. McAfee?"

"The man looked exactly like him." She shifted in her blanket and started to tear up. Detective Tremble needed to ask more questions but could tell this was all too much for her. He called her father to come and get her. He hugged her as he sobbed.

Jesse and I get to her house after leaving the cabin. I open my bag and empty the contents. I grab the journals from Mr. Elman's place and the one from the cabin and look at dates.
Claire went missing in 2018 around Valentine's Day. I look at the dated entries leading up to Valentine's Day and found this:

2/8/18

I MADE A MISTAKE. SHE'S GONE FOREVER. I GOT TOO DRUNK AND WE

GOT INTO AN ARGUMENT. I BASHED HER IN THE FACE WITH AN EMPTY BEER BOTTLE AND JUST KEPT HITTING HER. I COULDN'T HELP MYSELF. HER BLOOD WAS ALL OVER MY CLOTHES AND HER SKIN WAS ALL OVER THE JAGGED EDGES OF THE BOTTLE. I PUT HER IN THE CAR AND PUT IT IN THE RIVER. I USED A SMALL CINDER BLOCK ON THE ACCELERATOR. I CAN'T AND REFUSE TO GO TO JAIL FOR THIS. CLAIRE DESERVED TO DIE. SHE WAS IMPURE.... SHE CHEATED ON ME. THEY'LL NEVER FIND HER.

Then there was the photo album, it held horrors that no woman should see. It was photos of women being drugged and tied up. My heart broke when I saw the last set of photos. It was Leona, being tied up and she was laid on the floor. She had a gag in her mouth with her wrists and ankles tied. She's crying in the photo.

Chapter Nineteen: Tell No Lies

I still can't get that image of Claire's body out of my head. I shudder at the thought that it could've been Leona. I tell Jesse what I found and he looks at me with horror.

"Seriously? How did she escape?" Jesse asks incredulously.

"I don't know. Maybe we should ask her."

We go to my house and find Leona on the stoop of our porch. She's looking at her phone.

"Hey sis, I have a question."

"What's up?"

"Did you ever take photos for anyone?"

Her expression changed from happy to fearful. She started to bounce her leg and bite her lip.

"What do you mean 'take photos'?" she asked with air quotes

"I found a picture of you being bound. You were crying in the photo." I say, scared of what she's going to say next.

"I took a couple photos for an ex. Fucking perv." she explained. She was close to crying now.

"I'm sorry I asked you that.

"No, you're fine. It's just a part of my past I want to leave behind."

"I understand. Did he own a cabin by chance? Near the river?"

"Yeah, he did. Why?"

"That's where they found Claire Chesterfield's body."

"Really? You think he killed Claire?"

"It's a possibility."

After I talked with Leona, I found another manila envelope on the coffee table. I open it and it's a photo of Lila tied to a chair. Her head is stooped low and she's bleeding. In blue ink, it says, "Meet me at the Full Moon"

Chapter Twenty: The Ruse

Detective Tremble calls me and tells me that he has some information on Lila.

"Hey, we found some evidence that suggests Lila was kidnapped by Ezekiel McAfee."

"What? Our chemistry teacher?"

"Yes, he kidnapped her from Jesse Atterly's party."

"That can't be true."

I look back at the journals and they're both initialed E.S. not E.M., I feel sick. That man had Lila the whole time. He was at dad's recovery party. I hang up the phone with Detective Tremble and call Jesse.

"Hey, Jesse. I think I know who actually kidnapped Lila."

"Who?"

"His initials are E.S. not E.M."

"So, it's not our chem teacher?"

"No, but a close second. It's his twin brother. But the question is why?"

"I don't know. You're getting too deep into this. Maybe it's best to leave it to the cops."

"No, I'm not going to stop until I find Lila."

"It's going to get you killed, Mia!"

I hang the phone up and start to go through the journals again. See what I missed. I found an entry about me.

12/19/2021

MIA GOT AWAY. THAT LITTLE BITCH HAS WHAT'S COMING TO HER... SHE'S GOING TO REGRET EVER LEAVING. I'M GOING TO CATCH HER. SHE'LL NEVER RUN AGAIN. I NEED TO FIND A NEW PLACE TO "WORK" SO SHE DOESN'T HAVE THE COPS COMING HERE. I KNOW THE PERFECT PLACE. THE OLD DEVELOPMENT NEAR KNOCKNEE HILLS IS THE PERFECT PLACE. IT'S DESOLATE AND NO ONE CAN RUN BUT INTO THE WOODS. THERE I CAN FIND THEM

EASILY. MY LITTLE RABBIT WON'T BE GONE FOR LONG...'

Before I could read more, I felt like I'm being watched and I found a man across the street taking a photo of me. I google Knocknee Hills and find an old development that's just on the outskirts. The cabin is a ruse. That's not where he keeps his victims.

Chapter Twenty-One: Darlingwood

Darlingwood is the unfinished development near Knocknee Hills. It's filled with suburban houses and a cul de sac. I search the first two and find nothing. The one at the end of the cul de sac looks like it's being used. I check there. The house is half finished. The same smell from the cabin hits my nose. That smell of soot and rain.

I check the kitchen and there's nothing but used paper coffee cups and a coffee maker. I check the first bedroom and there's a closet

of women's clothes. They're all tattered and bloody. I take it these are trophies of his. I check the second room and there's a duffel bag laying on the floor.
I check it and there's an ax and a handgun in the bag with a devil mask and black clothing. I also see a desk with a camera. I check the desk and it's a bunch of photos of women being bound. Their eyes are pleading with the man behind the camera. These are his past victims.

I look for the basement. It's in the back of the house near the second bedroom. I go down the stairs and the smell of bleach hits me. Its strong ammonia-like smell burns my nostrils as I walk through the basement. I see a medical table in the middle of the room. It's got an IV pole next to it. There's a bag of saline hooked to the top. I look at the tray next to the bed and find a vial. It's GHB. It's a sedative, it must be what he uses on his victims. I feel sick and want to leave. I hear footsteps upstairs and I find a place to hide. I hide under the stairs and I hear a man's footsteps descending down them. My heart starts to race and my palms start to sweat. I have nothing to protect myself with. I knew I should've left as soon as I saw the photos. I look for the nearest exit and there's a backdoor in the corner of the basement. It has to lead outside.

I hear the man say, "Son of a bitch." and then he ascends the stairs again. I breathe a sigh of relief and bolt for the door. I open it and it's a hallway. It leads to the outside but there is a room to the right. It's the same place Lila was held. There's still blood splatter on the walls. It worries me that the blood could be Lila's. I check the room for anything that could lead me to her and I find test results from a clinic downtown. It's the results of a pregnancy test. It's positive and it has Lila's name on it. I take it and run towards the backdoor. That's when I hear a man say, "Get back here!" and I ran as fast as I could.

When I get home, I try to piece together what all of it meant. Why Lila would hide her pregnancy, why she got kidnapped. I read more of Lila's journal and found an entry from the night she got kidnapped.

10/31/23

I just found out that I'm pregnant. How am I going to tell Ezekiel? Where am I going to go? I don't want to ruin his career. I'm afraid he's going to kill me if he finds out. Plan B didn't work and now I'm going to have my teacher's baby. He told me he loved me but now he doesn't want anything to do with me. WHAT DO I DO? Our relationship started off casual. Then we started fooling around after hours in his car. We've been on multiple dates since '22. We've been together for over a year now. I hope he can accept this baby and we can run away together.

I'm dumbfounded and sickened. Why sleep with our chemistry teacher? I knew that wink meant more than kindness.

Chapter Twenty-two: Knock, Knock

I hear a knock at the door and Mama answers.

"Mia! Detective Tremble is here to talk to you!" she yells up the stairs.

I freak out and tuck everything under my pillow. I make it to my door and he's already knocking on it. I open the door and he sits at my desk. I forgot that there was a photo of me getting out of the taxi on the desk. I sit on my bed.

"So, how are you today, Mia?"

"I'm as good as I can be. How are you?"

"I'm tired, kiddo. Between the body and your friend going missing, I'm tired." he says, rubbing his eyes. They're bloodshot and it looks like he's been drinking. His breath smells heavily of alcohol. With his job, I don't blame him.

"What did you need to talk about?" I inquired.

"I need to know if you saw Lila with a man the night she disappeared." he says, folding his hands over his rotund belly.

"Yes, sir, I did. But I don't know what he looks like. He was wearing a mask." I answer.

"That's what I was worried about."

"Have you found her yet?"

"Yes, but she's in the hospital. She needs medical attention."

"How bad was she hurt?"

"I can't disclose that information. Mia, I need to find the man that did this." he says, getting up from my desk.

He walks towards the door and says, "Don't go where sleeping dogs lie." with that, he leaves.

As soon as he left, I felt relieved. Lila was alive.

Mama came up the stairs to my room. She asked me if everything was okay. I explained that Lila was alive and that she's in the hospital.

"Do you want to go visit her?" she asked

"Yeah, let me grab my bag." I answer

We arrive at the hospital and I ask what room Lila Atkins is in.

"I can't disclose that information. Mia, I need to find the man that did this." he says, getting up from my desk.

He walks towards the door and says, "Don't go where sleeping dogs lie." with that, he leaves.

As soon as he left, I felt relieved. Lila was alive.

Mama came up the stairs to my room. She asked me if everything was okay. I explained that Lila was alive and that she's in the hospital.

"Do you want to go visit her?" she asked

"Yeah, let me grab my bag." I answer

We arrive at the hospital and I ask what room Lila Atkins is in.

"She's in room I32 on the ICU wing." the receptionist said.

The ICU wing? This is bad. I hurry down the hallway to the elevator. As I'm ascending, I think the worst has happened. I get to the ICU wing and find her room. There's a man talking to her.

"You lost the baby?"

"Yeah. His brother was too rough with me, putting me in the trunk." she says, stifling back tears.

"Your plan didn't work out, did it?" the man says, patting her leg.

"No, our future is ruined." she concurred

"You had no future to begin with." he scoffed.

"How do you know?" she asked

"Because he's your teacher and you're the student. That was never going to work and you know it." he answered

Before he could turn around, I hid against the wall. Lila was beat up pretty bad and her right eye was closed shut. I walk down the hallway with my hood up and see the man leaving. I walk back up the hallway to Lila's room and find that she's crying. I knock and she tells me to go away. But I persist and come anyway.

"Lila, why didn't you tell me?"

"Tell you what? That I got pregnant by our chemistry teacher and I had hopes we would run away together?"

"That's why you got kidnapped?" I ask, looking at the girl that was once my best friend.

"It was part of the plan but it didn't go as planned. I guess that's what you get when your boyfriend's brother is a psycho." she laughs.

"He's the same man that kidnapped me, Lila. This isn't funny. I almost died." I scoff, thinking laughter would be the best way to keep from crying.

"Well, the plan was to get "kidnapped" then me and Ezekiel would run to New York. I would go to college and raise our baby girl." she said kidnapped with air quotes.

"I still need to find him and end this. He's killed so many women. He has to be stopped."

"I lied and told the cops that it was Ezekiel that kidnapped me."

"Why?"

"Because that bastard deserves time for what he's done." she says with a malicious smile. This is a smile I have never seen from her before. "His brother is a serial killer! He needs to go to prison! Not Mr. McAfee. All he did was get you pregnant and he didn't want to deal with it!" I exclaim, the nurses come down the hall to see if everything is alright.

"Yes, everything is fine." Lila lies, her expression changed from angry to relieved in just a matter of seconds.

Feeling betrayed, I leave the room. I've never felt so angry before. I start to piece everything together. Lila was obsessed with Mr. McAfee and got pregnant by him. Or did she?

Chapter Twenty-three:

Reconciliation

I called Jesse to apologize for hanging up on him the other night.

"Hey Jesse, I want to say I'm sorry for hanging up on you the other night. I was so caught up in trying to find Lila."

"It's okay, I'm just worried about you. Did the cops find her?"

"Yeah, she's in the ICU at Haven Point Medical."

"The ICU?? Is she okay?"

"She has a couple broken ribs and a black eye. There's something I need to tell you."

"What?"

"Lila orchestrated the whole kidnapping. She was a part of it."

"Seriously? What was her reason?"

"She wanted Mr. McAfee to get arrested."

"Why?"

"Because he didn't warrant her advances."

"I knew there was something strange about her."

"She borrowed the money from Connor to run away with Mr. McAfee."

"So the journal entries were fake?"

"Yes. Now the question is, why did she get harmed in the process?"

"Meet me at Witch's Brew in about twenty minutes."

"Sure. I'll be there."

I walk to town and make it to Witch's Brew. The smell of coffee and rose incense hit my nostrils as I walked in. I see that Lila is working. Her eye is still swollen shut and she's walking with a limp. She looks pitiful. I order an affogato with extra espresso and sit at a booth in the back of the cafe. Jesse comes in and orders a black coffee with no sugar, he's hardened the last time we spoke.

"Look, Mia, I'm sorry I got upset and didn't talk to you for a couple days."

"You're fine, sweetheart. In that time frame, I found where he keeps his victims."

"Where?"

"In Darlingwood."

"Darlingwood? That's just a skip from my house. Ugh, that gives me chills." he shuddered.

"So he doesn't keep them in the cabin?"

"No. I found a pregnancy test that belongs to her."

"A pregnancy test?? What were the results?"

"It said it was positive but I doubt it's real."

"Shit on a shingle. Do you still have it?"

"Yeah."

I pull the test out of my bag and show it to Jesse.

"That clinic has been closed for almost two years now." he says, looking at the header of the document.

"That's why I think Lila is doing this for attention." I surmise

"Attention?"

"Yeah, she wanted the attention of Mr. McAfee."

"Poor girl."

Lila storms over to our table and says, "She's lying! I'm really pregnant!"

All the patrons of the cafe are staring at her now. There's a silence that washed over the cafe. We just looked at her and continued our conversation.

"So, do you still want to go out with me tonight?" I ask, holding his hand.

He rolls his eyes at Lila's outburst and says, "Definitely. I'll pick you up at 7."

Chapter Twenty-four: The Truth

Detective Tremble comes into the interrogation room and sits, He's waiting for Ezekiel McAfee to be brought to him. Ezekiel is brought in by two guards. They sit him down in the chair adjacent to John's. He looks haggard and crazed.

"So, Mr. McAfee. Tell me the history between you and Lila Atkins."

"Well, she was 18 when we started dating, I swear. We started dating in '22. It was platonic at first and then escalated. She wanted more than I was willing to give."

"More than you were willing to give?"

"Yeah, I didn't want to pursue the relationship any further, detective."

"I see. So you decided to kidnap her to get the message across?"

"No, sir. I was visiting my father's grave the night she was kidnapped."

"I still don't believe you."

"Sir, I'm telling you, I had nothing to do with her disappearance." he says, shaking his head.

"Well, she told me that it was you that kidnapped her. You also tortured her." John says, putting his hands over his rotund belly.

"No, it was my brother. We're identical, he's a lunatic."

"Yeah, okay. I don't think you know how much trouble you're in."

"I know, but I'm innocent. We were separated as teenagers. I was adopted by Stephen and Adaline McAfee. My brother stayed with our biological parents. They lied and said that I was a troubled teenager and I don't know what else."

"Well, it might be that you're actually a troubled adult. I found your wall of torture, Ezekiel."

"I haven't lived in that cabin in over five years, I let him rent it. I live in Knocknee Hills."

"Yeah, sure. Do you have proof?"

"Yeah, you can get a warrant to search my house. It's 2212 Chandalay Drive."

"Okay." John takes note of this.

"I'm not even a real chemistry professor. My brother stands in for me while I work in my studio."

"Studio?"

"Yeah, I'm a photographer. Emil is the smart one. He took my place in several of my classes in college. He took all of my tests in chem. He even grades my tests for me."

"Hmm. That's new."

"Emil is a smart man but he's the troubled one. He liked to kill innocent animals and look up women's skirts when we were teenagers. He is a depraved psycho that needs to be stopped."

"Okay. We'll look for this body double of yours if there is one."

"He's not a body double, he's my twin brother."

"We're also investigating a house fire that happened about a month ago. We found a body in the basement. Can you explain that?" John says, raising his brow.

"What do you mean?" he says, looking dismayed.

"Stephen McAfee's house was burned to a crisp. They found charred remains in the basement. The man that lived there, James Elman, also had his car stolen." John says, thinking about the man in the hospital bed.

"Oh no, I thought he was kidding."

"What do you mean?"

"Emil actually killed Adaline."

"Actually killed?"

"Yeah, he killed her because she was abusive towards me and Stephen. Stephen was a sickly man, he had cancer. But she didn't care. She wouldn't feed him for days on end. She would beat me for little things like leaving a dish in the sink."

"Oh, cut the crap. Take him away, ya'll." John says, waving a dismissive hand. The guards take him away and he's pleading with him. They put him in his cell, John can hear the man's sobs down the hall.

John makes note of the address and tells his men to get the car ready. He doesn't care about formalities like a search warrant. He's gonna pin this son of a bitch if it's the last thing he does.

Arriving at Chandalay Drive, John notices the surroundings. Perfectly manicured lawns. Long, elaborate driveways. But Ezekiel's house is an eye sore. His lawn is overgrown, his driveway is cracked and crumbling. The house looks dilapidated in regards to the other houses.

Going in, he notices the photos on the walls. It's photos of dogs, families, and picturesque settings. *This guy really is a photographer,* thought John.

The house is an open concept. Like a studio apartment. He goes over to Ezekiel's desk and finds a photo. It's of Ezekiel and his brother standing side by side. They're identical. The only difference is one of them has a scar above their right eyebrow. Ezekiel's face is scar free.

He gets into Ezekiel's computer and finds photos of women being bound. One of them looks like Mia. But she's older. The title of the file is *BDSM: Gagged and Bound*. John feels wrong looking at these photos. He closes the tab and starts looking around.

Seeing there's nothing incriminating, he feels defeated. He knows that Ezekiel is going to get off scot-free. He needs to ask him about his brother's whereabouts.

"Let's go boys." he says.

The men leave. On the drive back to the station, John is filled with questions. *Why is he still in contact with his brother if he's a killer? Is he in kahoots with him? Or does he know the depraved acts he's been committing?*

Returning to the police station, John goes back to the interrogation room. He sits with his hands over his belly. He tells the men to grab Ezekiel one last time.

Ezekiel is brought in. His eyes are rimmed with red from crying so much. They sit him down and he begins to sob again. He puts his head in his hands.

"You can stop the water works. We took a look at your place." John says. He leans in and rests his elbows on the table. Ezekiel's expression lightens as he says this. He rubs his eyes with one cuffed hand.

"What did you find?" Ezekiel asks.

"Like you said, nothing." John says.

"I'm free to go?" Ezekiel asks.

"Yup. But don't think we won't keep an eye on you." John says, his eyes turning into slits.

"Okay. I'll stay away from my brother too, just to be safe." he says.

"Good idea. Can you tell me where he is?" John says.

"That I don't know. He could be in a completely different state by now." Ezekiel says.

"Alright. Well, if you see him, give me a call." John says.

****

Ezekiel gets taken to processing. He gets his wallet, phone, and other things back. His tears were not of lament, they were tears of rage. He's going to get that bitch back for what she did to him. She's going to pay.

Chapter Twenty-five: Double Vision

The night finally arrives and I put on my best clothes. I spritz my smoky cherry perfume and wear my braids down. I put on my lip gloss and brown lipstick combo, my eyeliner, and mascara. I'm ready for tonight.

"Mia! Your date is here!" Mama said

"Alright! I'll be down in a second." I grab my purse and I head downstairs.

Jesse is absolutely stunning. He's wearing a triple black suit with a purple tie. The purple really brings out the brown in his eyes.

"Hey cutie, you ready to go?"

"As ready as you are, handsome."

We head to Giovanni's, a beautiful Italian restaurant facing the river. We pull into the parking lot and get to the reservation booth.

"Two for Audley, please."

The man at the booth looks at us with curiosity and says, "Yes, let me show you your table."

Our table is right outside near the river. The patio is covered with fairy lights and candles. The atmosphere is uber romantic.

I pull Jesse's chair out for him and sit on my own. He looks absolutely handsome in this light. His olive skin glows and his black hair gives off a bluish hue.

"You look absolutely beautiful tonight, Jesse." I say.

"You don't look too bad yourself." he shoots right back.

"I like your perfume. It smells smoky and sweet." he says

"It's my favorite perfume. It's a dupe of Tom Ford." I say

"Nice."

"Your lips are so pretty." I say as I imagine myself biting the bottom one.

"Thank you. I think yours are very kissable." he says.

If I was a lighter shade, he'd see me blush. I hope this date goes well. I'm afraid I'm going to blow it. He's so handsome and I want to make him mine.

"Thanks." I smile

The waiter comes and asks us what we want. I order the carbonara and Jesse orders the risotto. We also get tiramisu for two. The waiter thanks us and we continue talking.

"So what's your favorite color?" Jesse asks

"Purple. How about you?" I say

"Red, the color of courage. I see that you like the color of royalty. I like that." he says

"What's your favorite book?" I ask

"The Outsider" says Jesse

"I love Stephen King. His writing is amazing!" I chime.

"What's your favorite book by him?" he asks

"Carrie. She finally got sweet revenge." I say

The waiter comes back with our food and we eat. We enjoy Italian cream sodas and share our tiramisu. The night is coming to an end and he still hasn't asked me to be his girlfriend.

"I've been meaning to ask you a question."

"Yes?" I say with a twinkle in my eye

"Will you be my girlfriend?" he asks

"Of course, Jesse. I'd love to be yours." I blushed

He hugged me and held me for a moment. Then he looked down at my lips, traced his thumb on my bottom lip and kissed me. It was the best kiss I've ever had. His lips tasted like strawberries. I kissed him again and we nuzzled noses.

After our date, we went to Witch's Brew. Lila was still working. She sees us and frowns.

"I see you love birds had a great time." Lila said as she saw us holding hands.

"Yeah, it was great."

"Good I guess. I don't appreciate you lying on me, Mia."

"I didn't lie, Lila. You're delusional and you won't admit it. You helped Emil frame Ezekiel for murder and kidnapping!" I raise my voice, unaware that Detective Tremble is right behind us.

"So Emil Santana is the man that kidnapped Lila?" Detective Tremble asked.

"Yeah, he also framed Ezekiel for the murder of Claire Chesterfield."

"Well, I be damned. How do you know this?"

I tell him about the journal entries and how the journal belonged to Emil and not Ezekiel.

"You're kidding me. You know you could get in trouble for withholding information."

"I know."

"Well, I have men patrolling your house just in case. Ezekiel got out today."

"Okay. I'll be safe going home."

"I'm not going to say anything, I promise. Just don't delve any deeper into this, or I'll have you arrested. Got it?"

"Okay."

We arrived at my place and mama was still up. She's drinking a cup of coffee, watching the news. She sees me walk in last, "Did you have a good night?"

"Yeah, it was fun."

"Did he ask you out?"

"Yeah."

"What'd you say?"

"Yes."

"That's good."

"Did you hear that evil teacher got out?"

"What? He didn't do it."

"He didn't? The police said all the evidence points at him."

"Yeah, well, his brother is the one that did the killings."

"His brother? I thought Mr. McAfee was an only child."

"Me too. Then I saw him and his brother at dad's recovery party."

"Detective Tremble said he got out and was looking for you."

"Don't worry, we're safe. Detective Tremble has men patrolling our street as we speak."

"We got protection of our own."

Leona says

She opens a cabinet and there's two pistols. A .32 and a .22 with man stopper bullets.

"Where the hell did you get those?" I ask

"I got them after I found out Lila went missing." she says

There's a knock on the door and she hands me the .22. I hide it in my purse and peek through the window. It's Detective Tremble.

"Ladies, everything will be oka-" before he could finish, he heard gunshots.

Chapter Twenty-six: Showdown

The gunshots were close and we all ducked.

"Get in the house!" Detective Tremble yelled

Detective Tremble closes the door behind me and fires two shots of his own. Leona and I are armed. We head towards the back of the house and see Ezekiel. He's got an ax.

"Stand down! I repeat, stand down!" says one of the officers.

The gunshots continue and he proceeds to walk toward the house.

We ran back inside, "Everyone get upstairs! He's coming towards the house!"

Jesse and Mama run up the stairs and stay in Mama's bedroom. Now it's time to fight this man. Detective Tremble is flanking the door from the inside. Me and Leona are standing at the stairway.

"Y'all ready?" Detective Tremble says.

We nod and have our guns at the ready. Ezekiel starts hacking at the door frame. "I know you're in there, Lila!" he says.

"If it weren't for you, my reputation wouldn't be tarnished!" he keeps hacking. He finally breaks through and Detective Tremble starts firing. Ezekiel swings and Detective Tremble's hand is cut severely. It's dangling by a few tendons.

"You're mine!" he yells in a blind rage. His eyes are glossy and crazed. He's baring his teeth like a wolf.

"You stay the fuck away from my sister, you pervert!" Leona cried The house started to shake and a disembodied voice howled, "You're going to pay for what you've done!"

"Claire? I thought he kill-" he says before the ax leaves his hand. It clatters to the floor. I see Claire, she looks more like a corpse now than an actual woman. She's floating about six inches off of the ground. She flies into me and I suddenly feel cold. I feel a searing rage coursing through me. I grab Ezekiel by the throat and begin choking him. With superhuman strength, his eyes begin to bulge out of the sockets.

"Let go of me, you bitch!" he cries.

My voice turns demonic, "You'll pay for what you've done!"

Then I send him flying across the living room. The pictures on the wall shatter from the impact. He charges at me but I dodge him. "NO!" he screams. I grab the ax and hack away at his face. His head begins to split and his body falls to the ground with a deafening thud.

Jesse and mama run down the stairs. They scream at the sight of Mr. McAfee's body. They look at me as if I had something to do with it.

Ezekiel is still alive somehow, probably some divine punishment. He groans and his body spasms. He hits his head on the floor repeatedly, as if he's seizing and his body stills again.

Detective Tremble just stands there in utter disbelief. He's speechless until Mama goes over to check the damage of his hand. It's salvageable but he won't be able to fire a gun again.
Jesse runs to hug me, I cry in relief to know my baby is okay.

Chapter Twenty-seven:

Aftermath

"In later news, chemistry teacher and serial killer Ezekiel McAfee was killed in a gun fight with officers last week. He was also responsible for the kidnappings of three high school girls." Jan said. Before she said anything else, Ophelia turned off the TV above the server line.

"I'm glad they killed the son of a bitch." a man said, drinking his coffee.

Emil walks in with a man and greets me.

"Hey. I remember you from Michael's recovery party. You work here?"

"Yeah, I've been working here since I got out."

"Got out? From where?"

"Westbrook."

"Ah, westbrook. I've been to that place. That's where they put my brother when I went to look for him the first time."

"Look for him? What do you mean?"

"I was looking for him to tell him that our biological father passed on. He died from cirrhosis."

"That's horrible. My condolences."

"But he got sent there because they found him strangling a rabbit in the backyard. He was a troubled teen."

"So when did you go into foster care?"

"When we were 13."

"I see."

"Well, his doctor told me that he wasn't suffering from any mental disorders. He just killed for the thrill of it. Dr. Edmundson mentioned he was a 'hedonistic' killer," he says, grabbing a menu from the host's booth. They sit at the high bar and order a cup of coffee.

"Is there anything else I can get you?" I say

"Yeah, umm, a piece of today's pie." he said looking at the pie case. Today's pie was a millionaire's pie. It's my favorite pie other than sweet potato. I grab it from the pie case and cut him a slice. I prepare it with whipped cream and a cherry.

"Looks great. Thank you."

"My pleasure."

Ophelia cries out, "No! Not my daughter! Not my sweet baby girl, oh god why?!"

I run to the kitchen and see her sitting on the ground near the sinks. She's cradling her phone and crying. She got the news. News that would change her life forever.

"What's wrong, Ophelia?" I ask, looking at her hand. She must have cut it when she got the news.

"My daughter was missing for two months. They just found her."

"Is she alright?"

"No, she's gone. My baby girl is gone!" she sobs, hugging herself.

I get down on the floor and hug her. She sobs into my shoulder. She repeats "my poor baby girl" over and over, I hug her even tighter. "Shit. Hey waitress!" Emil yells "Coming!" I let Ophelia go and help her up.

I come back to the server line and see that he made a mess. The coffee got all over him. I give him a towel to dry off with. I clean off the counter and get him another cup of coffee. He wipes off his hand and I see a scar on his palm.

Chapter Twenty-eight: Realization

He kept his hands in his pockets during the recovery party, I feel my throat constrict and my muscles tense up. There's no way this is the same guy that almost killed me a couple years ago. I go outside and I feel like my heart is going to explode. My breathing quickens and I can't seem to catch my breath. I'm having a panic attack. I pull my phone from my apron and call Dr. Edmundson.

"Dr. Edmundson, it's Mia. The guy that almost killed me is at Full Moon." I say, looking into the restaurant. Emil is walking toward the door with the same look he had when he kidnapped me. I ran toward the back of the building, trying to find a place to hide.

"Mia, calm down. How do you know it's him?"

"H-He has the scar on his left hand." I stammer. I can hardly keep my composure. My hands won't stop shaking.

"Okay, but didn't they kill the guy that did all the killings?"

"I hoped so. But he mentioned you."

"Emil Santana never had any visitors but his brother."

"Exactly my point. He mentioned that Ezekiel was a hedonistic killer."

"No. It was Emil that killed for the thrill. It was Ezekiel that took him here."

I hear footsteps coming toward me. It's Emil. I hide behind the other side of the building in an alleyway.

"Mia! I know you're here! No need to hide from me." he said pertly.

His footsteps quicken and I run toward the front of the building. I make it inside and tell Ophelia to call the police.

Dr. Edmundson is still on the line.

"Mia, are you there?" she asks with a concerned tone.

"Yeah, I'm still here. He just chased me around the building!" I say

"Did you call the police?" she asks

"I had my boss call the police."

"Good. Now go to the office and don't come out until the police get there."

I comply and go to the office. I sit in the office and finally sob. How did he find me? Who was that man he came in with?

Chapter Twenty-Nine: Mystery Man

The police got there and started asking questions. They leave and put an APB out for a "dead man". I came back to the server line to get my bag. The mystery man is still sitting at the counter. He grabs my arm.

"Mia, you have to leave town as quickly as possible. He came back to finish business." the man says, still holding onto me.

"I thought he got arrested too." I say, panting.

"No."

"Oh God, I need to warn my boyfriend." I wince. His grip is really tight, I feel my arm going numb.

"No, you need to leave town NOW." he growls.

"How did he find out I still worked here?"

"Lila Atkins."

"Seriously?"

"Yeah, she wants you dead."

"Oh no, I need to warn Jesse."

I grab my bag and head for the door. The mystery man says, "Be careful, Mia."

Luckily, one of the officers was still there. I ask him for a ride home. We arrive at the house and there's an ambulance. They wheel a woman out on a stretcher. Leona is standing there rubbing her arms, she's crying. Anger aside, I approach her.

"Mia, mama got hurt." Leona sniffles. She's been crying for some time. Her eyes are rimmed with red and her nose is running. I hug her and ask about what happened.

"I don't know, I just came back from the store. I found her lying on the floor and her h-head was b-bleeding." she sobbed. I hear mama call my name, "Mia Yvonne."

I ran to the ambulance and held her hand, "Yeah, mama?"

"I believe you now. That man exists. I'm sorry I didn't believe you before. I should've protected you. I-" before she could finish, she passed out. The EMT's put her in the ambulance and took her away. Leona comes to my side, holding me. "We need to get to Haven Med as soon as possible." Leona says.

"Let me go pack a bag real quick. I need to call Ophelia too." I say.

I dial the Full Moon Diner and Brandon picks up.

"Hey Brandon, it's Mia. Mama just got put in the hospital. I won't be in tomorrow morning." I say.

"Are you okay? I heard about what happened this afternoon." he asks.

"Yeah, I'll be okay. Um, can you put my tips in my locker for me? I left before tip out." I ask.

"I'll bring them to you at the hospital. Is she going to be on our side of the county line?"

"Yeah."

"Okay, I'll bring them to you."

"Thanks, Brando."

"Not a problem, kiddo."

I hang up the phone and get in the car. We got on the road and Leona's car stalls. She pulls onto the shoulder of the road near the woods. I see a man in the corner of my eye when we pull over. I'm reluctant to get out of the car. Leona asks what's wrong. I just point into the woods and there was no one there.

"There's nobody there, girl."

"I saw someone. He's here." I say, I feel my breathing quicken again. I look at the other side of trees when I notice Leona's eyes widen with terror.

"He's behind me, isn't he?" I ask.

Then I hear a tap on the window. It's Emil wearing the devil mask. He's tilting his head and smiling, "Come out, my little rabbit." He rounds the car and tries Leona's door. It's locked but mine isn't.

"Leona, you need to run as fast as you can. I can't let you get hurt like Mama." I say, opening my bag in the backseat. I grab the .32 from the night Ezekiel got killed. I put it in the waistband of my jeans. I lock my door before he rounds the car again. He tries my door and starts using the knife to jimmy the lock. Leona gets out of the car and runs down the road screaming for help.

His focus is on her for just a few moments. I kick the door open and he goes rolling down an embankment. I get out of the car and slide down the embankment.

When I get to the bottom, he's already scrambling to get up. I kick the knife out of his reach and put my foot on his chest. "You hurt my mama?!" I kick him in the face and get on top of him. I start throwing punches left and right.

He's not getting away with all that he's done.

He throws me off of him and spits out half of a tooth. He bares his teeth like a growling wolf. "You're going to pay for that, you little bitch!"

He gets up and starts running towards me, the chase begins.

I ran like I did all those years ago.

I ran as fast as I could. I felt like a rabbit being chased by a wolf. He is a monster that needs to be stopped. *Why am I running? He should be running from me. I'm not afraid anymore.* I slide to a stop and pull out the gun. When he comes to the clearing, he puts his hands up.

"Don't you move a single muscle. I'm sick of running from you!" I say, my hands still shaking.

"We can talk about this, right?" he says with his eyes wide and hands shaking.

"No, we can't. You're going to pay for what you've done." I say, aiming for his chest. I pull the trigger but it only clicks. He charges at me, tackling me to the ground. He hits me repeatedly and I start to lose consciousness.

When I come to, he's dragging me through the woods by my ankles. I try to scream but he's got tape over my mouth. My wrists are tied above my head. I drag my hands across the ground, feeling for something to latch on to. I grab the root of a tree and hold on tight. He tugs at my ankles, I kick him in the back and he goes flying down the dirt path. I get up slowly, my head is still swimming from the repeated blows.
I ran to the road and tried to find a ride to the hospital. A pickup truck rolls past and stops. It's Edna from the diner. I get in and

lock the door.

"What's wrong, girl?" Edna says, looking at me with concern

"There's a man chasing me." I say Emil hits the window before we take off. We head to the hospital and she drops me off. I get to the emergency room and ask the receptionist what room mama is in.

"Room 120." the nurse directs me down the hall. I run down the hall and find mama. She's sitting on the bed with a bandage on her temple. Leona is sitting at her bedside.

"Who did this to you?" I ask, holding her hand.

"It was a man in a devil mask. He came looking for you."

"I know, he chased me in the woods near here. I barely got away."

"He needs to be stopped. The police are still looking for him."

Mama tightens her grip on my hand. Tears well up in her eyes and she says, "Baby girl, I'm sorry for not believing you. I thought nothing could happen to my little girl." she kisses my hand and puts it up to her face.

"It's okay mama. I forgive you. Emil needs to be stopped. I'm the only one that can stop him." I say, taking my hand away.

I get up and start pacing, "Why is he still after me?"

Leona gets up and tells me, "Because you were the one that got away."

I was the first of his victims to get away. I didn't fight him even though I should have. I wasn't strong enough then. I didn't have the courage to fight back. I'm tired of running from him. If it's a chase he wants, a chase he'll get.

I give Mama a kiss on the cheek and head for the door. "Be careful, girl." Leona says, holding my shoulder, I hug her. I grab my bag from the hook and call Jesse.

"Hey, honey. I'm gonna need your help, mama is in the hospital." I say

"What?! What happened?" Jesse asks

"Emil got to her before I could come home from work. He was looking for me." I say, gritting my teeth. My heart is pounding and my hand is clenching the phone really tight.

"What do you plan on doing? Killing him?" he says

"I'm going to make him fear me." I say with conviction. He's going to pay for what he did to my mama. No one hurts my family.

Dad comes into the ER and is looking like a madman. He sees me and runs over. It looks like he's been crying.

"Is Winona okay??" he asks, his hair is in spikes like a cartoon character. His eyes are bloodshot and he's out of breath.

"Yeah, she's got a minor concussion. She'll be okay." I say as I put my bag on my back.

"Thank God. We may be separated but I still love her. You know that, right?" he says, slicking back his hair. Mama still loves him but she hasn't seen him since I was put in

Westbrook. She's afraid he'll be the same old, same old.

"Yeah, Dad, I know. You should go in and see her. It'll do her some good." I say.

"Where are you going?" he asks, looking me in the eyes. He can tell something is wrong.

"I'm going to find the man that did this. I know who did it." I say

"Who did this?" he asks

"Emil Santana."

"What? I thought he was dead. There's no way it could've been him."

"No, that was Mr. McAfee that got killed." I say, remembering the first day of class, he didn't deserve what happened to him.

"I have to go."

"I can take you, kid."

"Jesse is coming to pick me up. Love you dad." I say, leaving through the automatic doors.

Jesse is in the pick up patient bay in front of the ER. I get in and he looks like he's seen a ghost.

It's Emil and he's running towards the car. He tries to open the door but Jesse locked them as soon as I got in. He squeals out of the parking lot and we're on the road. Mr. Elman's car is right behind us.

He is in the driver's seat and he looks pissed. Lila is in the passenger seat. There is a man in the backseat of the car but I don't know who it is. Then I see the logo on the shirt. It's Dad.

Chapter Thirty: Wreck

"He's got dad! And Lila is with him!" I say, I feel myself starting to cry. My eyes are stinging with tears. I don't know what I'd do if he hurt my father. My dad is the only one on this earth that truly believed me. He was there the first day I was admitted. He was there when I had my first break up. He was there all this time.

Dad has a bag over his head and his hands are tied. I need to find a public place for Jesse to pull over. While thinking, Emil hits Jesse in the rear. We propel forward and skid to a stop. I hit my head on the dashboard. Emil crashes into the back of Jesse's car at high speed. We hit the guard rail and went rolling down an embankment. The same embankment I chased him down.

"Are you okay?!" I ask, looking over at Jesse. His head is at an awkward angle but he's breathing. I look down and my legs are fine. I can feel them. But I think my ankle is broken. Jesse groans and says, "What happened?"

"We've been in an accident. Are you okay?" I ask, looking to see where we are. We're upside down and my braids are hitting me in the face. I see the pistol I had, it's within reach. I grab it and get the magazine from my bag.

I get the knife from my bag and cut my seatbelt. I start sawing at the seatbelt and finally get free. I check my ankles by rotating them from left to right, they're both fine.

I'm ready to fight him. I climb the embankment and see Mr. Elman's car. My dad is still in the car but he's not moving. I run up the embankment and check his pulse. He's still alive but he's asleep.

I don't see Emil anywhere. Then I hear a thunderous crack in the air. He's got the whip. I take a deep breath and have the gun at the ready. I slide down the embankment and find him smiling. The same wolfish grin. He keeps his distance and yells, "You're not getting away this time!"

"You wanna bet?" I aim for his chest and fire twice. He falls to the ground and writhes in pain. I missed his vital organs and arteries. I did this on purpose. I want him to feel the pain me and mama felt. I walk toward him and kneel down. I stick my finger in his bullet wound and he screams.

"You feel that? That's only the beginning for you." I say, wiping the blood on his shirt. I grab the rope from when he restrained me and tie it around his wrists. I patted him down to check if he had any weapons and he had a knife. I take it and put it in my back pocket. I drag him down the path to the cabins and find an old hunter's hook. I find the pulley and ratchet it down. I hook it under the restraint and hoist him high in the tree. I grab the whip and dish out the same treatment he gave me. After each lick, he would scream out, "Let me go! I'm sorry!"

"Sorry?! You'll be condemned for all you've done!" I gave him one last lash and threw away the whip. I fall to my knees, screaming. He's not going to make it out of these woods alive. I'm going to make sure of it.

"Mia! What have you done?!" Dad says, his wrists were still bound but he managed to get the bag off of his head. He looks at Emil all beaten and bloodied. He looks back at me with the look of incredulity. I never felt so angry. I get up and hit the tree he's suspended from. My knuckles are bleeding. I hit it again.

"Dad, he needs to pay for what he's done." I say, my voice is trembling.

I cut the restraints off of Dad's wrists and he hugs me. "Honey, you need to get out of here before the cops come. Take that car and go as far as you can from here. Give me the gun and run." he says before letting me go.

"What are you going to do?" I ask him, handing him the gun.

"I'm going to finish the job. He needs to pay." he says with a tone I've never heard him use.

"Leave me here. I'll go to jail for protecting you. I'm sorry I didn't protect you all those years ago," he says, aiming the gun at Emil's head.

"Dad, don't do this. He should be the one going to jail, not you." I look in the front seat of Mr. Elman's car and Lila is gone. She's hiding behind a tree near the embankment. She comes out with a large branch and almost hits me. She slams the branch down onto the ground and grabs me by the hair. Screaming, I scratch at her hand but she's not letting up. She finally throws me to the ground and she stands above me. Wiping the hair from her face, she hits me.

She yells, "Yes, I did it for attention, so what? You were all they talked about for TWO WHOLE YEARS! Poor Mia this, poor Mia that. I was tired of hearing your name! You think you're so special because you were the one that got away! Well, let me tell ya, you're not! You're nothing, Mia. I got pregnant on purpose so some attention would be diverted to me! I felt like a nobody!"

I kick her in the knee and she falls. She groans in pain but gets up. I scramble to get up and I kick her in the chest. This time she stays down.

We go to Jesse's car and get him out. His leg is broken and so is his arm. We grab him under his arms and take him up the embankment. We put him in the backseat of Mr. Elman's car and headed back to the hospital.

Chapter Thirty-one: Happy Ending?

Emil Santana was found in the woods of Gorin Ridge. He was taken into custody by the FBI and the trial for Claire Chesterfield's murder is all over the news. He's killed 30+ women in the past twenty years. They found multiple bodies in the woods after he confessed to the other murders. Lila stayed in Hollow Hill and dropped out of college. Emil was given 24 consecutive life sentences. They found him bleeding out in the courtyard. A fellow inmate shanked him in the gut 14 times.

Jesse and I moved to Lexington shortly after this. We are still an item as of today. He proposed to me on our anniversary. We're planning on getting an apartment together soon. I'm going to school to be an English teacher and Jesse is going to school to be a biochemist. We're attending UK this fall.

Mama and Dad got back together, it's strange seeing them together again. But it's nice, I'm glad they're happy.

Detective Tremble got a promotion to lead detective and was awarded for his heroism. He still believes that I should study criminal justice instead.

THE END

Made in the USA
Columbia, SC
30 June 2025